"So, I guess paused to tak in his stoma stepped off the cliff a few minutes earlier in the hang glider. "So," he said again, hesitating, "what would you say to me taking you out to dinner to celebrate my first flight? We could go to Ports of Call on the Pier."

"Oh, Jed, that's awfully sweet of you to ask," Leslie replied, smiling. "But I can't tonight."

"Why not?" Jed blurted. Immediately, he was sorry he had asked. Even before Leslie answered he knew why. *And* why she was all dressed up now.

"I have a date with Jeff tonight," Leslie said softly. Any softer and she would have been whispering. "I'm sorry, Jed. You know I like you a lot as a friend, but I *am* going out with Jeff. I thought you understood."

Jed kicked some dirt with his foot. "Yeah, I understand. I guess in all the excitment I just forgot."

"Well, I'd love to go hang gliding with you again," Leslie said.

"Sure. Like I said, anytime," Jed replied, trying to hide the catch in his throat. Then he made himself busy by dismantling the glider. It was hard enough just looking at Leslie now, let alone speaking to her. As he shoved his equipment back in the van and tried to regain his composure, he wondered how, in the short space of half hour, he could have flown so high, and now feel so low.

Other books in the ENDLESS SUMMER series:

ENDLESS *Summer*

CHANGING GEARS
Linda Davidson

IVY BOOKS • NEW YORK

Ivy Books
Published by Ballantine Books

Produced by Butterfield Press, Inc.
133 Fifth Avenue
New York, New York 10003

Library of Congress Catalog Card Number: 88-91244

ISBN 0-8041-02557

Manufactured in the United States of America

First Edition: February 1989

For
Marcia Amsterdam
and
Lisa Howe
We're a team!

ENDLESS SUMMER
Changing Gears

Chapter 1

Even though it was real noisy with all the laughing and screaming in the beach house living room, Jed Mason almost wished he had brought a book downstairs to the party. Maybe then he wouldn't feel like such an extra wheel.

From where Jed was sitting, on the edge of the makeshift dance floor where his housemates and their friends were throwing themselves around to the music, he felt ill at ease and in the way. He swiveled his stuffed armchair around on its set of wheels and closer to the floor-to-ceiling window. Now he was facing away from the all the frenzied couples and toward the midnight-blue sky. He was now within earshot of the pounding surf. The

1

least he could do to make himself feel more comfortable was to get out of everyone's way.

Immediately Jed's eyes darted to the light from the flickering bonfires on the dark stretch of beach outside. Gazing out at the peaceful, moonlit seascape, he felt much more relaxed and a lot less like a piece of furniture to be tripped over in the middle of the dance floor.

For one thing, with his back turned away from everyone, Jed felt less conspicuous, almost invisible. Secondly, he didn't have to spend a whole painful evening watching Leslie Stevens, the secret love of his life, dancing the night away with her arms draped around the shoulders of her brawny boyfriend, Jeff Porter, head lifeguard at Marina Bay Beach.

If he had had enough sense, he would have stayed upstairs until the party was over rather than let Leslie torture him with her tanned, blond good looks and sweet, intimate smiles just for Jeff. But the potluck party food spread out on the dining-room table, the lasagna in particular, had lured him from his books. He hadn't even bothered to change out of his baggy, no-name jeans and white T-shirt.

"Come on, Jed, why don't you get up and dance?" Russell Stevens, his roommate and Leslie's equally good-looking brother, called out as he and his girlfriend, Pamela, whirled toward him.

"In a minute. I'm taking a rest," Jed shouted back over the din of the loud, taped music blasting from Leslie's boom box.

He eased back in his chair. Except for cruising the snack table and chowing down on several assorted doughnuts, pretzels, peanuts, chips, and anything he could get a handful of, he wasn't sure what he was taking a rest from.

He certainly hadn't knocked himself out dancing. Even if he could work up the courage to ask someone, by this time everyone was already paired off for the rest of the evening.

Russ's volleyball buddy Chris was bopping to the music with wild-haired Rain, a relief lifeguard who worked with Jeff and Leslie on Marina Bay Beach. Nick, a surfer who hung out with Fury, one of Jed's housemates, was monopolizing Erica, the high school volleyball champ. Danny, another surfer, already had laid claims to Erica's friend Maggie. And Pamela, Tracy, and, of course, Leslie already had boyfriends. No doubt about it, Jed was a third wheel.

It wasn't that he didn't want to join in the fun, but beyond stuffing his face, he really didn't know how or where to begin. And now it was way too late to even try to get something going with anyone. Besides, Jed knew that deep down, he only wanted Leslie, even though she'd seemed totally entranced by Jeff all evening.

The romantic tune now wafting from the boom box made Jed feel even more alone. Finally, he decided to get up and get something to drink. The salty snacks had made him awfully thirsty. He threaded his way between the slow-dancing couples and crossed the living room, deliberately avoiding looking at Leslie and Jeff, who were doing more than just dancing down the darkened hall.

Jed walked up to the counter that divided the kitchen from the dining room. A few nearly-empty plastic bottles of warm root beer and orange soda were all that were left. Jed plunked a couple of melted ice cubes into a Styrofoam cup and drained what was left of both root beer and orange into it. He stirred the drink with his finger, then took a sip. It was terrible, but he downed the concoction anyway.

"What's to drink?" Chris asked, coming up behind Jed. He had obviously worked up a thirst from moving to the music.

"Nothing now. I drank it all," Jed admitted.

"You're kidding."

Jed shrugged. "There wasn't that much left. I'll check to see if there's anything else," he offered.

Jed walked over to the fridge and took out

two remaining cans of Diet Coke. They were probably Pamela's. She was always on a diet and virtually lived on the stuff. He was going to ask her if she wouldn't mind contributing her sodas to the party, but Pamela looked much too preoccupied to care. Someone had dimmed the lights in the living room and lowered the volume on the boom box. Pamela and Russ seemed to be enjoying the romantic atmosphere on the couch.

"Thanks," Chris said, taking a cold can of soda. He slid open the door to the deck and stepped out into the moonlight to join Rain on the sand.

The party, Jed surmised, was taking a new, quieter direction. But he didn't mind the lull. No one seemed to notice him when he sat down at the dining-room table to doodle on a napkin with a felt pen he found in the pocket of his jeans.

Out of everyone's way, but still close to the food, Jed had a perfect place to work something out on paper: a carefully engineered drawing of the hang-gliding apparatus he'd been designing in his head all day.

He had only sketched a few lines of a pulley device on the napkin when he felt a yawn coming on. He stifled it, but he couldn't shake the tired feeling. Deciding to call it a night, Jed stood up and grabbed a handful of peanuts.

He walked quickly past the two couches, taking note that Leslie and Jeff had moved from the hall to the more comfortable couch opposite Pamela and Russ. Jed felt a pang in his chest and focused on the wall clock. It was only eleven. He popped some peanuts into his mouth and headed upstairs.

Why should he care if he cut out on the party early? It wasn't as if he'd be missed. Besides, it was Sunday night, and he had a big day watching seven-year-old Alex Hartman ahead of him. After being away from his little charge all weekend, Jed always found adjusting to Alex again every Monday a little rough.

As if he were tanking up for the difficult baby-sitting job ahead of him tomorrow, Jed stuffed the rest of the peanuts into his mouth and wiped off the excess salt on his jeans. He was beginning to feel a little sorry for himself and to look forward to seeing Alex. Even if the little rascal *was* a handful, at least he was someone to talk to.

Chapter 2

"Make a sand castle with me," Alex pleaded the next afternoon.

Jed rolled over onto his stomach and continued to read *A Guidebook to Hang Gliding*. He felt no guilt at all ignoring the pesky kid's request. He had already helped him make four sand castles today alone.

"Please, pretty please, Jed! Make one more with me. I promise this will be the last one."

"Come on, Alex, you sound like a broken record. You said that the last time. Give me a break. Can't you see I'm trying to read?" Jed answered without looking up from his handbook.

"You're always reading."

"And you're always making sand castles.

7

Don't you ever get tired of them? This will be the twenty-fifth one you've made this week, but who's counting?"

The skinny little carrottop shrugged. "So? That's the fourth book on hang gliding you've read this week. Don't you ever get tired of reading?"

Alex had him there. It was true that Jed had thumbed through three other books. But each one approached the subject from a slightly different angle. This one was the most technical. Besides, he couldn't bone up enough on hang gliding.

Any day now he was going to try out his new equipment. He had to be sure he understood how to rig and manipulate the glider correctly. Just from reading, Jed already knew that in this sport there wasn't much room for error. Right now he was studying the diagram he'd completed before picking up Alex this morning. He was planning to put together something makeshift in Russ's carport to get the feel of flying before taking a test flight off the bluffs.

"Okay, okay. You win," Jed conceded, putting down his book. If he didn't give in to Alex now, it would only be a matter of time before the kid got his way. Alex would keep on pestering him and, in the meantime, Jed wouldn't be able to concentrate. The sooner he built Alex a sand castle, the sooner he'd be imagining himself soaring through the air again. He scooted off his towel and down onto the wet sand where Alex had already excavated a network of canals to bring water to the storage holes he had dug.

Jed waited patiently while Alex, using the sand from the castle he had just demolished, reformed the base of sand castle number five. Then Jed dipped his hand into the water-filled hole and brought up a handful of soggy sand. As he drizzled it lazily through his fingers to decorate the base, the sun beat down on his back. Jed took comfort in the warmth of the afternoon sun and the fact that there were worse ways to spend the summer than being a mother's helper at the beach.

He could, for instance, still be in Berkeley. There the fog came in every morning in the summer, hung around until about three o'clock, lifted slightly, and returned for good an hour later. Or he could be working indoors all day at the computer store where he had had an after-school job during the year. But, worst of all, he could still be living at home, where his parents could nag him about his weight, about taming his shaggy, sandy, hair, or about his messy room.

He did, however, have Mom and Dad to thank for his summer job. His parents had gone to the University of California at Berkeley with Alex's parents. Although the Masons now lived in northern California, they had all recently met at a class reunion. His parents were the ones who had suggested to the Hartmans that their son might help them with Alex over the summer. Luckily for Jed, they had gone for the idea.

But he did have to give himself a pat on the back for landing a place to live at Seahorse Shores, the same beach complex in which Alex lived. He had simply loaded up his VW van with all his gear and driven down to Southern California a couple of days early to look for a room to rent. And he had nabbed one on the very first day after answering an ad in the *Marina Bay Beacon*. Rather than waiting until after five o'clock as the ad had suggested, Jed had arrived at the doorstep of 1521 Sandpiper Drive the first thing in the morning. He had also had the good sense to bring a couple of reference letters along, one from the Hartmans and one from the manager of Computerland. That had impressed the hell out of Russell Stevens. But, in all honesty, Jed knew that it was the first month's rent and the security deposit that he had handed over to Russ in cold cash that had sealed the deal.

So Jed couldn't sit around basking in the sun, the Pacific Ocean lapping at his feet, and complain that he was bored with sand castle construction. He was well aware that the alternatives were a whole lot less appealing. Besides, his summer, in most respects, was turning out just the way he had planned. After all, he *was* spending practically every day at the beach reading up on all the sports he hoped he would eventually get around to doing.

The only area of his life that wasn't going well, Jed admitted to himself as he dribbled some more wet sand onto the turrets, was his love life. He still hadn't met the right girl. Okay, he corrected himself, he hadn't met an available girl, period. But he wasn't all that concerned, at least, not yet. Most of the summer still stretched before him, as endless as the rows of girls in skimpy bikinis stretched out on beach towels all around him.

Jed reinforced a crumbling castle wall and, from behind his blue-tinted sunglasses, checked out three girls who were lying on their stomachs and working on their tans just to his right. One was wearing an iridescent blue bikini, another a hot pink and black monokini, and the third a zip-up-the-front, yellow-and-black one-piece made out of wet-suit material.

To Jed, the bathing suits were those girls' only differentiating features. With their long bronzed legs and long blond hair, all three of them looked equally terrific. The only problem was that not one of them had noticed him. If only one of the girls would glance in his direction, Jed was sure that he could get her interested. Once he impressed her with his vast knowledge of any number of subjects, he'd have her hooked. At the moment, he was almost an expert on how to hang-glide. What girl wouldn't be fascinated to hear him explain the secrets of powerless flight? He could even offer to take her along.

"Now look what you did, Jed!" Alex pouted. "You knocked down my bridge with your foot."

The whiny voice snapped Jed out of his reverie. "I'm sorry. It was an accident." He looked down to assess the damage. Sure enough, while he had been gawking at the girls and daydreaming about how to snag one, his foot had slid into Alex's bridge and destroyed it. "I'll build you another one."

"I liked *that* one! I want that one!" Alex appeared to be on the verge of tears.

"Look, Alex, be reasonable. I'll build you a better one with stronger walls and a moat," Jed offered.

Alex considered a minute. "Okay. But watch what you're doing this time. Promise?"

"I promise." Jed would have preferred to

watch the girls, but it was obvious that he couldn't do both and keep Alex happy. He'd have to restrict his girl watching until after working hours.

"Can I build with you? I'll let you use my pail and shovel."

Jed looked up and saw a chubby little kid with light brown hair and big ears holding a red plastic bucket. But Alex wasn't jumping to be friendly.

"Sure, sit down," Jed said quickly, taking an immediate liking to the pudgy kid. His roly-poly body reminded Jed of how he must have looked at that age. Alex eyed the kid's plastic bucket and didn't object.

"Thanks," the other little boy said to Jed. "My name is Mark."

"Give me your pail and shovel, Mark," Alex said. He obviously wanted it understood right away who was the foreman on this castle job.

"Okay," Mark said, handing over his toys and squatting down in the wet sand next to Alex.

Alex packed the pail with wet sand and turned it over, making the foundation for still another sand castle.

Jed was happy that Alex had lost interest in bridge building and didn't require his full attention. Although he wasn't able to get back to his book, Jed could at least do serious girl watching. The three females next to him had rolled over onto their backs. Now that Jed could see their faces, or at least the parts of them that weren't covered with colored zinc or sunglasses, he might be able to attract their attention. He hiked his blue bathing trunks over the small roll in his middle, raked his fingers quickly through his hair, and put on his best smile.

"There you are, Mark. You shouldn't just wander off without telling me where you are going," a voice scolded sharply. "I've been looking all over the beach for you."

Jed's view of the girls on the beach towels was now blocked by a pair of shapely, perfectly tanned legs. His eyes traveled from the legs to a flowered pink, aqua, and white bikini to a very pretty face. Like most of the girls on Seahorse Shores Beach, this one had that same winning combination: long, blond hair, bright, blue eyes, hot-pink lips, and an all-over tan.

And I've *been looking all over the beach for you!* Jed thought. So what if she looked like all the other girls? He had no problem with mass production.

"I'm sorry, Emily. I wanted to play with someone," Mark explained.

"Well, next time ask me first before you run off and start playing with a stranger," Emily chided him.

"Well, Alex is sure glad he did," Jed offered in Mark's behalf. "Why don't you sit down, Emily? The kids are having a good time together," he added, trying not to sound too excited.

"I can't. I left my towel down the beach," Emily said.

Jed picked up his own towel with the pink flamingos, shook off the sand, and spread it out again. "Here, sit down on mine," he said. Emily didn't appear to be all that comfortable about taking up his offer, but she sat down gingerly on a corner of the towel.

For the first time since Jed had started his mother's helper job, he wanted to kiss Alex. For once he was behaving and playing nicely with another kid. Maybe Alex would cooperate long enough for him to get to know Emily. Of course, knowing Alex's attention span, he couldn't take any chances on wasting time.

"So, do you live around here?" Jed asked for openers.

"In Pacific Pines. Do you know where that is?"

Jed shook his head. "Not really. I'm only here for the summer."

"It's the next town down from Marina Bay. It's pretty small. If you blinked as you drove past it on the freeway, you'd probably miss it. So where do you live during the year?"

"Up in Berkeley, near the university. But I'm working as a mother's helper in Marina Bay for the whole summer." Jed carefully drew out the words *whole summer*, wanting to make it perfectly clear to Emily that he wouldn't be here today and gone tomorrow.

But she seemed far more interested in where he had come from than where he was now. "Really? You mean where all the weirdos live? I've heard that Berkeley is crawling with nerds, dope dealers, and street people." Emily moved closer to the edge of the beach towel, fearing, Jed supposed, that he was one, if not all, of those types. If she had scooted any further away from him, she'd have been off the towel entirely.

Jed quickly decided that he wasn't going to make any points with Emily trying to defend his hometown. Berkeley was the kind of town that was impossible to describe to anyone who hadn't lived or been there. He quickly made up his mind to change the subject.

"I've just been reading a fascinating book on hang gliding," he said, hoping that Emily would ask him to tell her more about the sport.

"Hang gliding?" Emily raised her eyebrows. "Nobody I know is into hang gliding. What's so great about it?"

"What's so great about it?" Jed practically

shouted. "Did you ever stop to think that birds are no longer the sole occupants of the sky? That man can experience flight not only with instruments or engines, but by being solely supported by air?" He was getting all worked up just talking about how it must feel to fly.

"Not really," Emily answered, inspecting the bright pink polish on her toenails. "I'm not even sure I know what you're talking about. I'd rather go roller-skating or to the movies."

"How can you say that? Have you ever tried it?" Jed pressed.

"Not really. Have you?" Emily gazed out at the ocean.

"No," Jed replied, "but I'm planning to just as soon as I'm ready. I'm going to take my first test flight in a couple of days.

"Come on, Mark, we've got to go," Emily broke in. "Nice talking with you, Jed," she added, standing up abruptly.

Jed was not about to give up so easily. "Hey, do you have to go so soon? Look, the kids are really getting along well together now." Jed gestured toward Alex and Mark, who seemed happy as clams as they built their sand castle. Okay, so Emily didn't want to hear him talk about hang gliding. Well, he'd be glad to find something else to talk about: movies, music, baseball, politics, anything she might be interested in. If only she'd give him a chance, Jed knew they could get on as well as the two boys.

"Well, maybe they can play together again sometime," Emily replied. "Let's go, Mark."

"I don't want to go now. I'm having too much fun," Mark pleaded.

"I'm sorry, but we really have to go. I promised your mother I'd have you home by three. You can play with Alex tomorrow, if Alex wants to play with you," Emily said.

"Sure he wants to. Don't you, Al?" Before his little charge had a chance to say anything, Jed added, "We usually get to the beach around eleven o'clock. Why don't we all meet here for lunch? I'll bring some food."

"Yeah! I get to play with Alex tomorrow," Mark whooped.

"All right! A picnic!" Alex shouted.

"Okay," Emily agreed, far less enthusiastically than either of the two boys. She took Mark by the hand and started to walk away.

"You forgot your pail and shovel," Alex called out.

"Thanks, Alex," Mark replied, coming back to take his toys. "I like you."

"I like you, too, Mark. Bring your pail and shovel again tomorrow."

"I like you, too, Emily," Jed said in a high sing-song voice.

Emily frowned and, with Mark now firmly in tow, headed back down the beach toward her towel.

Chapter 3

Later that afternoon, Jed dropped Alex off and
sped into town. He was anxious to get into
Marina Bay to get some errands done, and it
was already four o'clock. But first he needed
to get something to eat—and fast. He was
always starving after a day with Alex. Turning
the corner onto Windward Way, he cruised the
van up fast-food row. Big decision coming up
on the right. Should he go for a Big Mac, a Big
Burger, or a Big Beef? he wondered, checking
the lines at the drive-thru windows. He
wouldn't have to wait at Big Boy.

"Thanks," Jed said to the guy in the red and
white cap as he took his Big Bag filled with a
Big Beef, Big Fries, and Big Gulp.

Now he was ready to tackle his hang-gliding

project. All he needed was to pick up the supplies to make his carport flight simulator work.

Jed pulled out of Big Boy and into Wilderness Supply, the outdoor sports store just up the street. He went straight to the mountaineering equipment counter and walked out of the store fifteen minutes later with everything he needed in one paper bag: parachute line, clamps, pulleys, and eyebolts.

One more stop at the supermarket to get food for tomorrow's picnic and he'd be shooting for home. He wanted to get started on his project while no one was around to distract him.

Jed wasn't the only boarder at Russell Stevens's beach house. After Russ had cracked up his brand-new Suzuki jeep, he had come up with a plan to rent out rooms to pay for the repairs before his parents came home from their vacation. Luckily for Russ, they were still in Europe. Angelo DeFurie, better known as Fury, a surfer from San Francisco, had rented the downstairs den. He worked nights as a backup bass player at a restaurant on the pier, but during the day he hung out with his buddies.

Fury's girl friend, Tracy Berberian, was from Fresno, and they sang country and western together. Tracy had a job at T-Shirts for Two on the main drag in town, and Jed figured she'd be working there now. Tracy shared a bedroom with Leslie, who wouldn't be home from the beach until at least six.

It was entirely possible, however, that Pamela Easton, who had rented out Russ's parents' master suite, might be around. But that presented no problem for Jed. She usually spent her afternoons sunning herself on the upstairs deck. Most likely she was out somewhere with Russ. As of last week, the two of them had become a hot number.

Jed sighed, thinking once again that everyone in the house was going with someone except him. Wouldn't it be tidy if he and Leslie became a couple? Jed turned off the highway and into the Seahorse Shores complex. Pairing up with Leslie was out of the question. He'd have to continue keeping feelings for that girl under control. Of all the blond, blue-eyed Southern California beauties on the beach, Leslie was far and away the prettiest in Jed's eyes. She seemed so much fresher and more vital than the others somehow, maybe because she was so toned and tanned from swimming.

Jed pulled up in front of the Stevens's weathered, redwood beach house, determined to get Leslie, and girls in general, off his mind. It was a waste of time anyway.

He went around to the back of the van and snatched up his groceries for tomorrow's picnic. Something just might work out with Emily. So what if he couldn't find the right subject to talk to her about? Maybe bringing lunch was a better approach. *Stop it,* Jed scolded himself.

He headed into the house and unpacked the groceries as quickly as he could, more anxious than ever to get started on his project. He looked around downstairs, and peeked into the bedrooms just to make sure no one was home. Then he went into the room he shared with Russ and hauled his hang-gliding equipment bag out of the closet. Finally, he went back to the carport and got his tools and supplies from the van.

Using a ladder he found against the side of the carport, Jed screwed eyebolts into position on the overhead beams. Then he quickly threaded the parachute line through them and attached some pulleys to the line. From his equipment bag he took out the steering bar, assembled it, and suspended it about four feet off the floor.

Now Jed was ready to rig the harness. He stepped back to inspect his work. Once again he'd amazed himself. The makeshift flying device had turned out exactly as he had engineered it on the little piece of paper in his pocket. But would it work? There was only one way to find out. He released the clamp, lowered the harness to the ground, and strapped himself into a prone position. Then he gave the line a pull.

"It works! It works! I'm a genius!" Jed whooped as he felt himself rising off the ground. He pulled the clamp up tight and used the steering bar to move back and forth through the air.

"I fly through the air with the greatest of ease," Jed sang loudly as he swung through the carport. He couldn't wait to step off the bluffs and soar like a bird on the air currents above Seahorse Shores Beach. Then he remembered the drop to the beach below and momentarily lost his nerve. But on his next pass through the carport, Jed assured himself that there was nothing more to hang gliding than what he was already doing. The only difference was that he'd be a little higher off the ground. Again he pictured himself taking off from the bluff, and this time he controlled his fear. He was ready!

"I'm a genius," he shouted again as he took another practice run through the carport. The only thing he needed to master now was getting down. He released the clamp, lowered his feet, and simulated a perfect landing. Beginner's luck, he thought, pulling himself up to the top of the carport for another try.

But this time Jed ran out of luck, beginner's

or any kind. The line snagged in one of the pulleys and he was caught hanging upside down from the ceiling. He tried yanking the line, but it wouldn't budge. Then he pulled on the steering bar to try to unjam the line, but the more he pulled, the more tightly the line jammed. Don't panic! Jed cautioned himself. Just jiggle the line gently and it will free itself. Still nothing happened.

"Help!" he shouted in desperation. "Help! I'm pinned to the ceiling of the carport!"

Then he remembered he was wasting his breath. Hadn't he checked carefully enough to make sure that no one was home? "I'm an idiot," Jed now mumbled to himself. He wondered if anyone held a record for hanging upside down, and if so, what it was. Glancing at his Casio he decided he might as well time himself in case he happened to break any records.

Ten minutes later Jed looked at his watch again. He was no longer interested in breaking records. All he wanted was to get down. How long would it take before he died from hanging like this? He strained to see out of the carport and glimpsed the paperboy riding past on his bicycle.

"Hey! I'm in the carport!" Jed shouted.

The paperboy glanced in his direction, tossed a paper onto the sidewalk, and rode on. Obviously he hadn't heard him.

Jed checked his Casio one more time. The good news was that it was now a few minutes before six. Leslie and Tracy would be off work and heading home soon. But how could he be sure that either of them would come straight home? It would be just his luck that they'd have dates after work. As for Pamela and Russ, if they were out together, there was no telling when they'd return. He closed his eyes. If no one arrived home soon, his last wish would be that he die peacefully upside down in his sleep.

"*What's that?*" Leslie shrieked, pulling into the carport suddenly in the Suzuki.

"Leslie, thank God you're home! It's me, Jed! I'm caught up here!"

"Jed?" Leslie jumped out of the car. "What in the world are you doing hanging from the ceiling? How'd you *get* up there?"

"Just get me down and I'll be more than glad to answer any questions."

Leslie put her hands on her hips. "Any suggestions how?"

"Stand on the bumper of the car and untangle the line. It's jammed in the pulley."

Leslie climbed up the jeep. As she worked on freeing the line, Jed wondered miserably why it had to be Leslie, of all people, who had to see him like this. This wasn't the way he had wanted to impress her. But maybe he shouldn't complain. At least he had gotten her attention.

"I think I've got the line free," Leslie called out.

The next thing Jed knew, he was sliding down, heading for a landing on the hood of the jeep.

"Perfect!" Leslie said, obviously trying to keep from laughing.

"Hey, it isn't funny. I could have died up there!" Jed protested.

"Would you mind telling me what you were doing up there?" Leslie asked, still chuckling.

Jed wriggled out of the harness and smoothed his hair. "I rigged up this crazy device to practice hang gliding."

"You mean to practice hanging," Leslie corrected him with a smile.

"You should have seen me before I got caught up there," Jed replied defensively. "I was flying across the carport like a bird. Now I'm ready for a test flight off the bluffs."

"This I've got to see!" Leslie said, raising her eyebrows.

"Really? Do you want to?" Jed asked excitedly. What a stroke of luck!

"Well . . ." Leslie backtracked.

"You mean it?" Jed asked.

"Oh, I don't know," Leslie replied halfheartedly. "When are you planning to try out your hang-gliding equipment?"

Jed tried to sound casual. "When do you have some time off?"

Leslie hesitated. "Tomorrow afternoon."

"Great! That's exactly when I was planning to take my first test flight. Why don't we meet back here around three o'clock and we'll drive up to the bluffs together?"

"Okay." Leslie nodded. "You're on."

"It's a date," Jed said enthusiastically.

"Well, I wouldn't go so far as to call it that," Leslie replied, heading toward the house. Suddenly Jed felt as if he were hanging on the ceiling again. When was he going to stop making a fool of himself?

Chapter 4

As Jed dismantled his flying device, he realized that he had just doubled his odds of getting a girl friend. If he didn't impress Emily on the beach tomorrow morning, he still had a pretty good chance of making points with Leslie in the afternoon. So what if Leslie had a boyfriend? Jed asked himself. Okay, so the macho hunk of a lifeguard was a hard act to follow. So what if an overweight nerd like Jed Mason couldn't hold a candle to Jeff? What did he care? As soon as Leslie saw him step bravely off the bluffs and soar into the air, she wouldn't be able to resist him. What girl could? A lot of them, Jed leveled with himself.

As he headed into the house, Jed felt as if tomorrow couldn't come fast enough. To make the evening pass more quickly, he fixed himself some dinner and got ready for bed early. He was glad that Russ still wasn't home. It was just as well that the house was quiet. He wanted to read over his books again for a while. Besides, the sooner he fell asleep, the sooner it would be morning.

The sun shining brightly into Jed's bedroom woke him up early. He rolled over and checked his Casio on the bookcase between the twin beds. It was only eight o'clock. Great! He had plenty to do this morning. He got out of bed and dressed quickly and quietly. Russ was sleeping soundly next to him. Jed had rarely seen him up and about before noon.

Although he dressed hurriedly, Jed took special pains to make sure his socks matched. Usually they didn't, but today was special. If something worked out with either Emily or Leslie, he'd even consider getting a decent haircut. In the meantime, he decided to wear his black-and-aqua Jams today. They were much more flattering than the short blue trunks he had worn yesterday. Sneakers and a black T-shirt completed his outfit. He had heard that black made a person look thinner.

Jed walked into the bathroom, wondering whether Russ would mind if he borrowed some of his styling gel. Russ would probably appreciate his going ahead and using it rather than having Jed wake him up to ask. Jed took the tube out of the medicine chest and rubbed some of the gunk into his hair, giving special attention to the cowlicks. Ordinarily they stuck up at the crown of his head as if they had a mind of their own.

Jed hesitated. Would Russ care if he also borrowed some of his aftershave lotion? He splashed some on, then headed downstairs to put together his breakfast and lunch.

"Well, *you* look all dolled up. Big date for this time of day, huh?" Tracy asked in a practiced Western twang.

In her tight black jeans, high white boots, Western-style shirt, and fringed black suede vest, Jed thought Tracy looked pretty done up herself for just selling T-shirts all day.

"Why the fancy outfit?" he asked, curious.

"Oh, I'm singing tonight at Ports of Call and I won't have time to get back and change. But what's your excuse?"

"I just felt like it," Jed said with a shrug. There was no point in mentioning Emily to Tracy, not until it was a sure thing. But he felt more confident now. If Tracy had noticed the extra attention to his appearance, Emily was bound to, also.

"Well, I've got to be moseying along," Tracy said, gulping down some juice. "I'm having breakfast at the Surfrider Cafe before I open the store. Have fun." She hurried out the door.

Jed glanced at the clock. It was already eight-thirty. He was due at the Hartmans' to pick Alex up at nine. He'd better get a move on, too. He took the ice chest out from under the counter and tossed the makings for hero sandwiches and some fruit and cold drinks into it. He had planned to make the sandwiches ahead of time but it was too late now. Once he had some cold cereal and a banana under his belt, he made tracks to the van and over to Alex's house.

As he stood in front of the Hartmans' door, waiting for Alex to answer the bell, he wondered what he would do if he managed to impress both Emily *and* Leslie. No problem, he told himself. If push came to shove, somehow he'd learn how to juggle two girl friends at a time.

"Look what I've got, Jed," Alex sang out as soon as he opened the door. "A red plastic pail and shovel just like Mark's. My dad bought it for me last night."

"Why didn't you get a different color?" Jed asked. Two identical sets of sand toys would mean trouble.

"That's the only color they had at the store," Alex explained.

"Well, maybe we should put your name on

your stuff so we can tell them apart," Jed suggested.

"No," Alex said, stamping his foot. "I don't want any marks on my new pail and shovel. See, I even took the price tag off." He held out the pail, then he looked at Jed with a puzzled expression. "Your hair looks funny. And you smell funny, too."

Jed could already tell what kind of mood Alex was in. He had spent enough time with the kid this summer to know that the best way to handle Alex when he was acting this way was not to say anything at all.

"Go get your sandals on and let's go to the beach."

Alex skipped off, then returned to the door with his pail still in hand and tan water sandals on.

"Good morning, Jed," said Mrs. Hartman, coming up behind her son. "Here are two towels, Alex." She handed them to the little boy to carry. "Alex tells me you're planning on a picnic today. Anything I can contribute?"

"I don't think so, Mrs. Hartman," Jed replied politely. "I think I've got everything. Ready to go, Alex?"

"Yep. Bye, Mommy," Alex said, clutching the towels in one hand and his new toys in the other. Jed was relieved to see that Alex seemed in a better mood now.

"Have a good time today, Alex," said Mrs. Hartman. "I should be back from work around two-thirty, Jed, so I'll see you both then."

"Okay, bye, Mrs. Hartman," Jed answered, leading Alex down the front path.

Although the beach where Jed and Alex had hung out yesterday was within walking distance, Jed decided to drive because of the heavy ice chest. A few minutes later, he pulled up at the Seahorse Shores Beach parking area.

"Okay, let's go," Jed said, hefting the ice chest up on his shoulder. Alex trailed behind him to the water's edge without complaining.

By the time they had plunked everything down in the sand, spread their beach towels, and gotten out of their shirts and shoes, it was already ten o'clock. Jed was glad that the day was perfect for a picnic, not a cloud in the sky. Alex entertained himself nicely for quite a while with his pail and shovel. And Jed had forgotten to bring his books along.

Even though the sun was quite warm overhead, it was still too early for the shapely sun worshippers to take up their tanning positions. Jed knew that they wouldn't hit the beach until later in the afternoon, so he occupied himself watching the Windsurfers try to catch what little wind there was in their colorful sails. The majority of them were spending more time in the water than riding on their boards.

Their unsuccessful attempts reminded Jed of the day not too long ago that he had talked Leslie into giving him a windsurfing lesson. As with many of the sports he had tried so far, he had had his share of beginner's luck. With Leslie's sound instruction he had stood up and ridden out to sea for several minutes. But eventually he had lost his balance, falling off his board and meeting the all-too-common, Windsurfers' wet fate. Leslie had really been a good sport and had praised him for his efforts. And that was that. But today was going to be different, Jed thought. He was trying an incredibly daring sport. Leslie *had* to take notice!

Why was he carrying on about Leslie? Jed wondered. Emily was due any minute. He thought about how pretty both of the girls were, Leslie with her clean-cut good looks, and Emily with her finer features. But now he'd better put Leslie right out of his mind, especially with Mark and Emily, this time with a beach towel under her arm, strolling toward him.

"Look what I've got!" Alex shouted, holding up his new pail and shovel the second he spotted Mark.

"And look what I've got," Emily said, removing a bottle of sunscreen from inside her yellow and white striped beach towel. Mark plopped himself down next to Alex in the wet sand, and Emily sat on her own towel, not nearly as close to Jed as he would have liked.

"And look what *I've* got," Jed said, opening up the ice chest. "Anyone ready for lunch?"

"We're not. We just got here, Jed," Emily reminded him.

"Well, why don't I start making some sandwiches anyway? By the time I'm through, maybe you'll be hungry."

"Whatever," Emily answered. She went to work applying sunscreen everywhere on her body, except where two tiny pieces of printed pink cloth covered her in the name of a bathing suit. Then she lowered her sunglasses to the bridge of her nose and stretched out on her towel.

Jed was too busy spreading mayonnaise on pieces of bread before topping them with ham and cheese to be upset that Emily wasn't paying much attention to him. What did he care if she spent some time sunning herself? he thought. The day was still young. Unfortunately, so were the kids.

"That's my pail," Mark screamed suddenly.

"No it's *not*. It's mine. Yours still has the price tag on the bottom," Alex pointed out.

"No, it doesn't. Yours does," Mark insisted, picking up a handful of sand and throwing it in Alex's face.

The next thing Jed knew, sand was flying onto the bread and into the mayonnaise jar.

"Stop throwing sand, you guys. What's going on, anyway?" Emily popped up when some sand stuck to the lotion on her stomach.

"Alex has my pail," Mark informed her.

"Let's see the pail," Jed said, trying to arbitrate the dispute. Mark handed the bucket over to Jed, who turned it upside down.

"Mark, I don't think he does. See, your pail still has a price tag on the bottom, and Alex took all his tags off," Jed explained calmly.

"Alex has my pail. Alex has my pail," Mark was hopping up and down.

"Mark, stop acting like a brat," Emily said, obviously fed up by now. "If you can't play nicely with Alex, we'll have to play somewhere else."

"I don't care. I don't want to play with him anymore. I want to go somewhere else. But first I want my own pail back."

"It's not your pail," Alex shouted at the top of his lungs. He was launching into a tantrum and kicking sand all around.

"Let's go, Mark," Emily said, grabbing up her towel. Mark snatched a pail and shovel set. Jed was certain it was the one that belonged to him.

"Maybe we can try again tomorrow," he said in desperation.

"I think this was a bad idea. It isn't going to work out. Come on, Mark, let's take a walk," Emily said, extending her hand.

Mark turned back toward Alex. "Good-bye crybaby."

Alex whirled around on his knees like a mad dog and threw another handful of sand in Mark's face.

"You deserved that. You provoked him. Now let's go," Emily scolded, yanking Mark by the arm. Good-bye hopes of getting anywhere with Emily, Jed grumbled under his breath as she and Mark marched quickly away from wild-eyed Alex. Jed sighed. Emily was probably feeling pretty relieved that Mark and Alex had had a fight. She was probably looking for some excuse to dump me anyway, Jed told himself, feeling really rejected. The kids' argument over the pails was an absolutely perfect reason to get out of the picnic. But how could Emily have been so sure that things wouldn't work out? Jed wondered. Why wouldn't girls even give him a chance?

Chapter 5

"I *know* it was your pail and shovel," Jed said as he drove Alex home at exactly two-thirty. "Still, you didn't have to have a fit over it."

"I'm sorry, Jed. I promise I'll be nicer next time."

At first Jed was skeptical. He had heard countless similar apologies before. But when Alex lowered his head and shuffled into the house, Jed was pretty sure that this time the little kid was genuinely ashamed of himself.

"I don't know if there will be a next time," Jed said. "Now Emily doesn't want Mark to play with you." So what if he was rubbing it in and making Alex feel even worse? An hour earlier he had wanted to kill the kid for ruining his chances with Emily. And having to eat sandy sandwiches hadn't improved his disposition, either. While he had gotten over most of his hostility toward Alex, he still wasn't feeling all that sorry for the brat now.

"Well, maybe I'll meet another kid tomorrow," Alex said hopefully.

"Tomorrow's Saturday. I won't see you until Monday," Jed reminded him. *Good*! he added to himself.

"Well, Monday, then," Alex corrected himself, obviously undaunted. After dropping his little charge off, Jed decided that he should be as optimistic as Alex. So they had blown it with Mark and Emily. Didn't Jed still have his date, or whatever she wanted to call it, with Leslie to look forward to this afternoon? Jed stepped on the gas and drove like a maniac the two blocks back to the house.

When he reached the driveway, he took a comb out of the back pocket of his Jams and slicked his hair into place again just in case Leslie was already home. He couldn't afford not to make a good impression on her this afternoon. Not that the way his hair looked really mattered all that much, Jed realized. He'd soon be wearing his hang-gliding helmet, which would probably mess it all up again. The helmet! he now remembered. He'd forgotten to put it into the van. He raced inside the house with the ice chest, dropped it off in the kitchen, and ran upstairs. On his way back, he ran into Leslie.

"I'll be ready in a sec," she told him. "I just want to change. Meet you at the car," she called over her shoulder. Jed climbed into the driver's seat and waited nervously. Now he had bigger things to worry about than his love life. For starters, he'd soon be jumping off a cliff, a stunt that he didn't exactly perform everyday. Where did he come off thinking that his test flight in the carport simulated the real thing? And even that practice session, he hated to admit, had ended in disaster. Even worse, after yesterday, he couldn't afford to have Leslie witness another failure. Then there was, of course, the reality of what failing to land safely back on top of the bluff and dropping three or four hundred feet to the beach below actually meant. That was definitely the last thing Jed wanted to think about now.

Fortunately, at that moment, Leslie bounced down the front path in a peach sundress. Her flowing blond hair and the full skirt of her dress shifted from side to side as she ran. The sight of her immediately took Jed's mind off less pleasant thoughts. Leslie had changed into something pretty and feminine just for him!

"This should be fun. I'm glad I'm coming along!" Leslie exclaimed as she climbed into the van. She smoothed her skirt carefully.

"That makes two of us," Jed said, feeling a surge of renewed confidence.

As he pulled away from the curb and headed up the windy backroad that led to the bluffs above Seahorse Shores Beach, he felt his heart quicken as it pumped adrenaline to all his muscles. Not only was he about to step off the bluffs and soar like a bird in the air, but Leslie was sitting right next to him!

Then, when Jed reached the flat plateau where the hang gliders took off, parked the van, and saw the sheer drop to Seahorse Shores Beach, he wondered why he hadn't begun his flight training by running off a smaller hill, or maybe even a sand dune. Why, he asked himself as he and Leslie got out of the car, had he decided to go straight to the top? From all he had read, however, he knew that there really wasn't much difference in the actual manuevering of the kite. One book had even said, Jed remembered, that gliders like his were very responsive to control and could be landed in a small area with relatively little experience. So what was there to worry about when he had the whole top of the bluff as his landing field?

"I don't know much about hang gliding, but is there anything I can do to help?" Leslie asked as Jed took out his equipment bag and started to assemble his glider.

"Yeah. Tie a blindfold around my eyes," Jed kidded. But deep down he was pleased that at last he had hit upon a sport that he knew more about than Leslie.

"What are you doing now?" she asked as Jed rigged the wing wires to the nose of the sails. He explained the secrets of rigging the glider as Leslie listened intently. It was just like her to not want to be a novice for long. After watching him this afternoon, Jed was sure she'd want to try it herself the next time out.

But right now it was his turn to shine. After he had attached the crossboom, the steering bar, and the harness and had double-checked to make sure all the fittings were secure, there was nothing left for Jed to do but put on his helmet and take off.

"Are you sure you're ready?" Leslie asked as Jed strapped himself into the harness.

"Ready or not, here I go," Jed shouted. Then he took several running steps, the last one off the cliff and into thin air. Behind him Leslie sucked in her breath in disbelief.

Jed, too, was caught breathless for several seconds before his bright orange sail filled with air. The next thing he knew, he was clutching his steering bar, more for security than direction. Forcing himself to look straight ahead, not down, he flew over the beach and out over the ocean. He felt like

Icarus as he headed toward the bright sun. Jed warned himself not to fly too high or too close to the big yellow ball, or his wings might melt and like Icarus's, plunge him into the sea. He put the thought out of his mind. Finally, deciding he had gone far enough out for his first trial flight, he leaned his body to one side and banked the glider into a turn. Then he centered himself again, rolled out of the turn, and headed back to terra firma.

As if he were a bird about to set down on the ground, Jed floated above the bluff, gently lowered his feet, and came in for a landing, just as he had practiced it. Then he tore off his helmet and harness, stepped away from the glider, and waited for Leslie to run and fling her arms around him.

"Oh, Jed, that was beautiful! Really beautiful! I'm really proud of you," she greeted him. She did run toward him, but that was it. No hugs, no kisses, no "my hero." "Are you going to try it again?" she asked.

Jed winced. "Once is enough. I don't want to stretch my luck."

"What was it like? You looked so peaceful fluttering above the earth."

"I guess it's as close to being like a bird as I can ever imagine."

"Were you scared?" Leslie persisted. "My heart was in my mouth for you the whole time."

"Only when I stepped off of the cliff," Jed replied. "After that, I pretty much went on automatic. My brain took over and I didn't have time to be frightened."

"Do you think you could teach me how to hang-glide?"

Jed had been waiting for Leslie to say that. And he was ready with an answer. "Sure. When would you like to start?"

"Oh, I don't know. I'll let you know when I have some free time, okay?" Leslie answered vaguely.

For someone who had sounded so eager at first, Leslie didn't seem to be jumping at the chance to learn now. "Anytime," Jed said. "Just let me know when." He hoped his voice sounded casual.

Now, Jed thought, was the perfect opportunity to get something going with Leslie. She had been sufficiently impressed with his hang-gliding accomplishments, and he didn't want to let the fact that she had gotten all dressed up for him go to waste. "So, I guess we should head back down." Jed paused to take a breath, feeling more butterflies in his stomach now than he had when he stepped off the cliff. "So," he said again, hesitating. "What would you say to me taking you out to dinner to celebrate my first flight? We could go to Ports of Call on the Pier. Tracy and Fury are singing there tonight."

"Oh, Jed, that's awfully sweet of you to ask," Leslie replied, smiling. "But I can't tonight."

"Why not?" Jed blurted. Immediately, he was sorry he had asked. Even before Leslie answered he knew why. *And* why she was all dressed up.

"I have a date with Jeff tonight," Leslie said softly. Any softer and she would have been whispering. "I'm sorry, Jed. You know I like you a lot as a friend, but I *am* going out with Jeff. I thought you understood."

Jed kicked some dirt with his foot. "Yeah, I understand. I guess in all the excitement I just forgot."

"Well, I'd love to go hang gliding with you again," Leslie said.

"Sure. Like I said, anytime," Jed replied, trying to hide the catch in his throat. Then he made himself busy dismantling his hang glider. It was hard enough just looking at Leslie now, let alone speaking to her. As he shoved his equipment back in the van and tried to regain his composure, he wondered how, in one half hour, he could have flown so high, and now feel so low.

Chapter 6

Jed slumped into the house a little after seven. To add insult to injury, Leslie had asked him if he would mind dropping her off at the pier where she had arranged to meet Jeff. "Oh, no sweat," he had replied, as if he looked forward to delivering her into her boyfriend's waiting arms. Why, he wondered as he traipsed down the hall, his equipment bag slung over his shoulder, had she even bothered to go anywhere with him at all?

"Leslie told me you were going to try out your hang glider today. How'd it go?" Russ asked just as Jed was about to go upstairs. He and Pamela were hanging all over each other on the couch in the living room. Jed really wasn't in the mood for chitchat just now. And seeing Russ, the six-foot volleyball jock and male version of Leslie, didn't improve matters, especially when his beautiful girl friend was lovingly raking her long fingernails through his sun-bleached hair. The last thing he needed to do now was hang around with a cute, cuddly couple. He'd rather go to his room to sulk, or, even better, sleep. Maybe he wouldn't wake up at all. That was how down he felt tonight.

"Okay," Jed replied finally.

"This I can't believe," Russ said, sitting up. "Jed Mason, the guy who never shuts up, is into one-word answers. I mean, hanging over the Pacific with nothing to prevent you from doing a nosedive into the water must have been better than just 'okay.' Come on, Jed, be a little generous with the details."

Jed sighed. It wasn't Russ's fault he was so miserable. "Well, to tell you the truth, it really was beautiful. It was almost like an out-of-body experience." He remembered all too well now how wonderfully weightless his pudgy, out-of-shape body had seemed. Maybe he should have left it forever.

"It sounds like a fabulous spectator sport," Pamela said. "You'd never get me to do it, but I'd love to watch you sometimes," she added.

"Sure. Anytime." He'd said that line before, and recalling to whom didn't help his mood any. Looking for a way to make a polite exit while there was a lull in the conversation, he excused himself. "I think I'll head upstairs."

But Russ didn't brush off easily. "What's the big rush, Jed? We're just sitting around, thinking about what to do for dinner. Why don't you join us?"

"Nah, thanks. I'm really pooped," Jed answered.

"When Jed Mason is at a loss for words *and* skips a meal, something's got to be very wrong. Come on, Jed. Sit down and take a load off your feet. Why the long face? You can talk to us. We've all cried on your shoulder when we had problems," Russ reminded him.

Jed had to admit the offer was very inviting. Why not pour out his troubles to Russ and Pamela? It was true that he had helped them both out when they needed him, Russ when he was having difficulty collecting rent from Fury, and Pamela when she had had family problems.

Jed plunked down his equipment bag on the beige carpet and plopped into a soft chair opposite the couch.

"I've had a really bad day," Jed began without any further prompting from either Pamela and Russ. "Actually, it all started yesterday." He went over how Alex had befriended Mark, how he had met Emily on the beach, then told

Russ and Pamela why Emily had walked out of his life as quickly as she had entered it.

He debated whether he should tell them how Leslie had unwittingly rubbed salt into the wound this afternoon, but decided against it. In the first place, he should have known better than to get his hopes up. It wasn't as if he hadn't known the score all along. He had just conveniently forgotten it.

"So, she's not the only pebble on the beach," Russ said sympathetically. "There are plenty more girls out there just like her."

"You don't have to remind me," Jed replied glumly. "That's exactly the problem. There are lots of girls on the beach, all right, but not one of them will give me the time of day."

"Now wait a second, Jed. So you weren't successful with Emily. But what have you learned from that?" Pamela asked, taking a more analytical approach.

"That I can't get anywhere with women."

"Now you're generalizing," Pamela pointed out. "Just because you had one bad experience doesn't necessarily mean you won't do better the next time."

"Oh, yeah? You want to put money on it?" Jed said. "Let's face it. No woman in her right mind is going to give someone with my body a second look."

"Well, looks aren't everything," Pamela told

him. "Anyone with any brains themselves can tell you're really smart."

"She's right," Russ added.

"Oh, look who's talking. Miss America and Mr. U.S.A.! It's easy for the two of you to say that. But think about it. What if, besides my brains, you had my body?"

Russ looked Jed straight in the face. "Oh, no, anything but that," he joked.

"Thanks a lot!" Jed sank deeper into his chair.

"Wait a second! I've got it!" A broad smile creased Russ's tanned face as his deep blue eyes lit up. He jumped up from the couch and started pacing.

Jed figured Russ must have had something really brilliant if he was that willing to untangle himself from Pamela. "Who says you have to have that body forever?" Russ went on excitedly. "What if you went on a shape-up program? You know, Jed, if you had the body to go with your brains, no girl could resist you."

"No way! You're *not* going to get me dancing around to one of those workout tapes!" Jed protested. "The next thing you know, you'll have me wearing a leotard."

"No, no, that's not what I had in mind. I meant something more like a body-building program. I could lend you my weights. In a couple of weeks you could look like this."

Russ winked and struck a bodybuilder's pose.

"Oh, so that's your secret!" Pamela teased, obviously admiring the biceps bulging out from under the sleeves of Russ's T-shirt.

"Well, volleyball also helped develop my upper body," Russ bragged, striking another pose that accentuated the muscles in his chest.

"Look, Russ, be serious. I can't look like that in a couple of weeks," Jed objected.

"If you went on a diet along with the program, I'm sure you could do it," Pamela assured him.

"And I'm not going on one of your weird diets, either. The first three letters of diet spells *die*. And that's exactly what would happen to me if I ate carrot and celery sticks like you do all day. I'd starve to death."

At the moment Pamela was wearing a blousy camp shirt and baggy white linen pedal pushers, so only her pencil-thin legs showed. But she was clearly as skinny as a model on the cover of *Vogue* magazine. She also had the high cheekbones, white skin, and gorgeous face to go with her svelte body. She was beginning to look a lot healthier these days, though. Russ had been working on putting a little muscle on Pamela, too. He decided to consider Russ's idea, but as for Pamela's plan, he still needed some persuasion.

She was up for the task. "I wouldn't expect a growing boy like you to live on rabbit food," she said. "The diet you should follow is very sensible. It includes all of the basic food groups, but no junk food."

"Tell me I have to give up bread and water, but not junk food," Jed pleaded. "I love that stuff."

Pamela shook her head. "You don't have to give up bread or water. In fact, you increase your water intake. It makes you feel full. You eat three balanced meals a day, and you can eat all the raw or cooked vegetables you want."

"Oh, yippee! What a treat!" Jed said sarcastically. Now he was even less certain that he wanted to go on Pamela's diet program. But he felt much better now, thanks to Russ and Pamela's concern for him.

"I'll need some more time to think about going on the diet, Pamela, but I'll definitely take you up on working with the weights, Russ," Jed said.

"Great," Russ replied. "They're in my closet. Anytime you feel the urge to lift five, ten pounds, help yourself," he offered.

"You really should consider the diet, Jed," Pamela urged. "Exercise alone won't take that extra weight off."

"Okay, okay. You win. But all this talk about

food is making me hungry. Weren't we going to think about what to do for dinner?"

"We were, but now that you've agreed to put yourself on a diet, I've got an even better idea. Why don't I cook you a low-cal dinner to get you off on the right start? We could have some grilled fish, a salad, some broccoli, and fruit for dessert," Pamela said enthusiastically.

Jed thought about the unappealing lean cuisine Pamela wanted to prepare. The two sandy but thick ham-and-cheese sandwiches with mayonnaise that he had had for lunch now seemed mouth-watering in comparison.

"Oh, boy! When do we eat?" Jed said in jest.

"Well, if Russ puts up the coals and you set the table, dinner should be ready in about an hour," Pam said seriously, heading into the kitchen.

"Can't I choose my last supper?" Jed pleaded. "Even condemned men get to pick what they're going to eat before they die."

"You're not exactly dying, Jed," Russ assured him. "When Pamela and I get through with you, you'll look like a new man. You'll be so trim and handsome that the girls will be falling at your feet. You'll have to push them aside just to get by."

Jed tried to imagine how he'd look in a bathing suit without his puffy cheeks, paunchy middle, and chubby thighs. Then he pictured himself on the beach surrounded by a throng of great-looking girls, all clamoring to get close to him. Without another word of protest, he marched straight into the dining room and began to set the table.

Chapter 7

When Jed's Casio alarm went off at six-fifty on Saturday morning, he immediately felt around under his covers for the digital watch to shut it off. He didn't want the electronic noise to awaken Russ, who was fast asleep in the other twin bed. The next thing Jed did was to pull up his striped pajama top and check his waistline. Even after one diet dinner, he did, indeed, feel a little thinner. But seeing was believing. Sure enough, his double roll looked a little less flabby than usual. He sucked in his stomach as far as he could to get an idea of how he would look thin, but there was still too much flab hanging over the elastic of his pajama bottom to tell. He wasn't exactly wasting away, he told himself, at least, not yet. Encouraged, nevertheless, by his slightly lighter feeling, Jed crossed the room and rolled a pair of dumbbells out of Russ's closet. If he got up early every morning for the next couple of weeks, and worked out, sticking to Pamela's diet at the same time, he was sure that he could drop a significant amount of weight pretty quickly.

He leaned over and tried to pick up the dumbbells, one in each hand. The weights thunked to the carpeted floor. He knew it! He should never have gone on Pamela's diet. Eating the way she had suggested, if you could call what he had had for dinner last night eating, had already sapped all of his strength! Who was he kidding? Jed scolded himself. What strength? Admit it, Jed! *You're in worse shape than you thought. You're a one hundred-and-seventy-five-pound weakling!*

Using both hands to pick up one dumbbell, Jed was finally able to lift it off the floor. He let go of the weight with his left hand and tried bending his elbow with just his right. After moving his arm back and forth twice, he was all tuckered out. He switched the dumbbell to his left hand only to discover that he could do even less with that one. *That's enough exercise for one day, thank you,* he thought. Hadn't he read somewhere that you shouldn't overdo things on the first day? He had already worked up a healthy sweat and earned himself a refreshing shower. He grabbed the dumbbell with both hands again to carry it back over to the closet. Thud! It crashed to the floor.

"What was that?" Russ shouted, jolting upright in his bed out of a sound sleep. "An earthquake?"

Jed sighed. "No, a dumbbell. I'm sorry, Russ. I didn't mean to wake you up."

"What time is it?" Russ rubbed his hands over his face in an effort to wake himself up.

Jed checked his Casio. "Seven."

"A.M.?"

"In the morning," Jed acknowledged.

"Right. Now would you mind telling me what you're doing working out with my weights at this ungodly hour of the day?"

"I was too excited about getting started on the body-building program to sleep. I figured the sooner I began, the sooner I'd shed some weight."

"Okay, okay," Russ broke in. He glanced out the window. Although it was quite early, it was already a sunny day. Russ shrugged. "As long as I'm awake this early, I might as well stay awake. Then I can fit in ninety, maybe, a hundred games of two-man volleyball. Why shouldn't I hit the courts at eight in the morning? It's a perfect day for it." Russ yawned and stretched, then hung his feet over the side of the bed. He slipped on a pair of beige, corduroy OP shorts, raked his fingers through his tousled hair, and walked over to Jed.

"Here, let me show you how to pick these things up." Russ bent down and lifted the dumbbells, one in each hand, off the rug as if they were toothpicks. Jed's jaw dropped almost to where the weights had been.

"You want these back in the closet?" Russ hefted the weights above his head. Standing there bare chested, he looked to Jed like the strong man in the circus.

Jed nodded his head in amazement. "How did you do that?" he asked.

"Easy. It's all in the legs," Russ explained, still holding the weights high.

"Let me try again," Jed said eagerly. "Maybe I can do it, now that I know the secret."

"No, Jed," Russ answered firmly. "You'll kill yourself. Actually, it's a good thing you woke me up. You're not supposed to start off with twenty-pound weights." He lowered the two bars to the ground and placed them gently down on the carpet again. "I need to change the weights for you. Ten pounds is all you should be lifting to start."

"You mean ten pounds is all I can lift," Jed corrected him. Russ removed the set of ten-pound weights from the rear of his closet, not bothering to contradict him.

"See what you can do with these," Russ said.

"That's much better," Jed admitted as he lifted one ten-pound weight off the floor, then flexed his arm several times before he had to put the weight down again.

"That looks about right for you," Russ said. "I want you to practice lifting one weight now, then two. When you feel comfortable lifting both of them, let me know. Look, I'm going to take a shower now, so I'll see you downstairs."

Russ grabbed a pair of yellow Jams from a drawer, snatched up his boat shoes, and beat Jed to the bathroom. To pass the time until Russ was through, Jed worked out with the one weight for a little while. Later he went downstairs for breakfast.

Leslie and the smell of sizzling bacon greeted him as he entered the kitchen.

Although it was Saturday, Jed figured from the way Leslie was dressed that she was on lifeguard duty today. He also knew that she usually got one weekend day off, so she most likely wasn't working tomorrow. Jeff had probably already asked her to spend the day with him, but, maybe, he hadn't and Jed could beat him to it. He began to think about how he could talk Leslie into spending Sunday with him. But she interrupted him before he came up with anything.

"I'm making some bacon and eggs for Russ and myself. Can I throw anything in the pan for you while I'm at it?" Leslie asked.

"Just one egg, thanks," Jed replied, tucking in his stomach.

"Only one? Are you on a diet or something?" Leslie looked surprised.

"You guessed it." Jed was delighted that Leslie had picked up on the hint. It made no difference to him if Leslie was going out with Jeff. Why couldn't he still try to get her interested in him? He knew, of course, that it would take everything he had—his brains, his personality, his sports equipment, and soon, he hoped, his brawn—to woo her away from him. So what? If he succeeded, having Leslie as a girl friend would more than make up for the time and effort he had put into winning her affections. Besides, Leslie had broken up with Jeff before. She might decide to do it again.

"Well, good for you," Leslie said simply, and went back to frying the eggs. That was all she had to say until later, when they were all sitting around the breakfast table.

After Leslie and Russ had chowed down their bacon, eggs, toast, and hash browns, Jed sat staring at the lonely egg on his plate, waiting a while before eating it in order to make it last longer. Finally Leslie put down her fork and brought up a new subject.

"I don't know what got you up so early this morning, Russ," Leslie said, "but it's nice to have a chance to talk to you before I have to leave for work."

"The dumbbell woke me up," Russ interjected, grinning at Jed. Jed grinned back.

"What's that supposed to mean?" Leslie asked, frowning.

"Never mind. It's a private joke. Go on," Russ said, with a wave of his hand.

"Well, last night Jeff asked me to deliver a message to you. He wants to challenge you to a full-court volleyball game. You and whoever you want versus the lifeguard squad. He needs an answer this morning."

"Whoa! I guess Jeff didn't like getting bageled in that two-man game Chris and I played against him and Rain yesterday. This must be his way of attempting revenge. Terrific!" A devilish gleam flashed in Russ's blue eyes. "This could be a real good time. Let's see, who'll I get for my team? Chris will want to play, of course, and the girls' high school champ Erica. Her friend, Maggie, is almost as good. With me, that makes four. Who else?" Russ thought a moment. "How about you, Leslie? It's hard to find a guy who's any better. That makes five. And picking up one more jock on the beach should be a snap."

"Jeff also said to tell you that he doesn't care what studs you come up with, he's still going to whip your butt." Leslie made her voice sound low and kind of macho, like Jeff's.

Although Jeff's invitation, Jed figured, was

probably motivated by his embarrassing fifteen-to-nothing loss to Russ, Jed also knew that it was in Jeff's nature to be pretty chauvinistic. He wouldn't expect Russ to choose any women for his team. It was, in fact, Jeff's patronizing attitude that had gotten him into trouble with Leslie earlier in the summer. The senior lifeguard had literally snatched a rescue out from under Leslie, and later he had taken all the credit for it. When Jeff explained to her that he had thought she wouldn't be able to handle the rescue herself, Leslie had become quite incensed and had broken up with him. But the big hairy guy had managed to charm his way back into Leslie's life. In spite of Jed's setback with Leslie yesterday, knowing that she had broken up with Jeff once kept alive his hopes of someday getting her to be his girl friend. What did she see in that guy, anyway?

"What about me?" he piped up. If Leslie was going to be on the team, he'd take up volleyball this instant, even if he had to read a million books on how to play it. He'd do anything to be on a team with her. The more opportunities he had to be near her, the better his chances of eventually winning her over.

"You, Jed?" Russ said, looking a little shocked. "Sorry, buddy, but . . ."

"I hate to hurt your feelings, big brother,"

Leslie broke in, "but you'll need two more players. I'm playing for the lifeguards."

Russ shrugged. "Okay. No hard feelings."

Jed remembered exactly when Leslie's strong loyalty to her fellow lifeguards had been formed. It was the night of the grueling lifeguard relay race at Torrence Beach. Leslie had furiously swum the last lap of the race in the dark. When she had emerged from the water, having won the race and clinched the trophy for Marina Bay, her teammates had hoisted her on their shoulders. Even Jeff had come around to congratulate her and to apologize for his chauvinistic behavior. Then they had gotten back together again. But, to get back to the matter at hand, what about his playing for Russ's volleyball team? His housemates seemed to have forgotten that his feelings could be hurt.

But Russ, Jed soon found out, wasn't totally insensitive.

"Hey, wait a minute, Jed. You've given me a great idea. Sure, my team of jocks could beat the lifeguards, no sweat. But if I took a bunch of wimps—I mean, novices—and turned them into a winning team, the victory would be even sweeter."

Jed noticed that Leslie looked puzzled. That made two of them.

"What do you mean?" she asked.

"Okay. I'll explain. First of all, Leslie, you can tell Jeff when you see him that I accept his challenge. And, second of all, you can inform him that Jed, Fury, Tracy, Pamela, myself, and Chris, if he's willing, will make up my team."

"Are you serious, Russ?" Jed asked in disbelief.

"Sure. I can shape you all up into a fine team. Once you know a few secrets, volleyball's an easy game."

"What secrets?" Leslie blurted out.

"Oh, no. I'm not about to reveal anything to the enemy," Russ replied mysteriously. He turned to Jed. "Just remember, my man, winning isn't everything. It's *almost* everything. Besides, the exercise will be good for you. What do you say?"

Jed nodded. Russ's enthusiasm was catching. He saw himself with a new body, one developed from playing volleyball, that Leslie wouldn't be able to resist. "You can count me in. But I don't know about Pamela."

Russ winked at him. "Don't worry. You just work on your game and your weights and leave the girl to me. I know exactly how I'll work on her."

Chapter 8

After Russ and Leslie had rushed out of the house, Jed sat for a while by himself at the dining-room table. Russ, Jed supposed, was anxious to get in his hundred or so two man games before the sand got too hot. He'd also heard Russ telling Leslie as they went out the door that he couldn't wait to have a good laugh with Chris over Jeff's boast. He probably wanted to get out of doing the dishes, too. Jed figured that between Jeff and Chris, the news of the big volleyball challenge would be all over town before Russ finished his first game.

Then Jed wanted to kick himself when he remembered that he hadn't gotten around to asking Leslie what she was doing tomorrow. Maybe later, he thought, as he started loading

the dirty dishes into the dishwasher, he'd ride
into town and find out. On second thought, he
was glad he hadn't gotten a chance to say
anything yet. Before he asked Leslie out, he
wanted to have an activity for the day in
mind—one she wouldn't dream of turning
down.

Now he was motivated to clean up even
more quickly so he could thumb through his
books for some ideas. Hurriedly he wiped
down the kitchen counter and dining room
table with a sponge, scrubbed out the frying
pan, and put the butter and milk away. Actually, he didn't mind cleaning up after everybody. Leslie had made the eggs and toast, and
Russ the hash browns, while he had done
nothing. It was also true that he had eaten
practically nothing, but as he walked upstairs,
he tried to tell his growling stomach that it
was in its best interest.

Back in his bedroom, he took a sports
encyclopedia down from the bookshelf and
sat down at Russ's desk. He opened to the first
"A" in the book: "Abalone Diving."

"These huge delicious gastropods were the
staple of California coastal Indians for centu-
ries, and archeologists have found abalone
shells in digs dating back to the fourth cen-
tury. Today the best abalone diving in California can be found at Abalone Cove just north of
the Channel Islands," Jed read.

That was it! Abalone diving! What an exotic, exciting sport! And Abalone Cove was less than an hour's drive up the coast.

Jed quickly skimmed the rest of the section. To his delight he discovered that he already had most of the equipment: diver's mask, fins, snorkel, wet suit, hood, gloves, even booties. The only things he was missing were an abalone iron to pry the abalone off the rocks and a game bag. He'd probably also need a fishing license, but he could get that and the other two items at Wilderness Supply in town. Then he had another stroke of genius. While he was at it, he'd rent Leslie a whole set of equipment and surprise her with it. She could hardly say no.

He snatched his wallet and car keys off the night table and dashed out to the van. On his way into Marina Bay he thought of several more good reasons for going diving.

For one thing, he'd be wearing his wet suit, which was tight-fitting and held in his stomach. But best of all, he actually knew how to skin-dive. His father had taught him how when he was a kid during several summer vacations they had spent in Maui. Wouldn't Leslie be surprised to see him cutting through the water like Lloyd Bridges?

Jed turned into the Wilderness Supply parking lot on Windward Way and pulled into a parking space. This time he headed to the dive shop. An hour later he was back outside, his arms laden with a woman's wet suit and other assorted skin-diving paraphernalia. In the pocket of his black Jams was his new fishing license.

Once back behind the wheel of the VW, Jed wondered whether he should head down to the beach to Leslie's lifeguard station and ask her about tomorrow now. Since he'd already gone ahead and rented the equipment, he decided he'd better. If she couldn't go, he could drive right back and return it and probably get some, maybe all, of his money back.

He drove down Windward Way to where it met the pier. As he stepped onto the beach near Russ's hangout, sure enough, there was Russ on the second court, setting up balls and practicing spikes with Chris, his lanky, curly-haired volleyball buddy. They were obviously waiting for the first pair of victims to challenge them to a game.

"Hey, Mason, where are you going? Want to work out with us?" Russ called.

"I can't," Jed replied. "I'm on my way over to see Leslie." He turned to Chris. "Has Russ had a chance to ask you about playing on the team?"

Chris nodded. "Yep. I'm definitely in. I wouldn't miss this challenge for the world. I just hope Jeff can round up some decent players. Otherwise, the whole thing will be a joke."

"Well, let's not get too cocky there, old buddy," Russ warned. "Let's hope the joke's not on us and Jeff ends up getting the last laugh."

"Come on, Russ. With you two hotshots on the team, we can't lose," Jed said.

"Thanks for the vote of confidence," Russ replied, "but we'll all need to get in a lot of practice—and soon. Chris and I can't do it alone, not with Jeff and his team out for blood," Russ said, sounding far more realistic than Jed about the abilities of his players. "When I get back to the house," he went on, "I'll talk to the others and set up a practice schedule. I'll let you know when we start our workouts."

Just then Chris, obviously wanting to get Russ's attention back on the court, set up another spike for his partner. Russ automatically leaped into the air to smash it.

"Way to go," Jed said, waving good-bye to Russ and continuing in the direction of Leslie's tower.

"Hi," Jed called up to Leslie when he reached her lifeguard station. So intent was she in looking out for weak swimmers in the water that she didn't hear him at first.

"Hey, Leslie," he shouted again.

This time he caught her attention. "Oh, hi, Jed. I didn't know you were planning on coming to the beach this morning."

"I wasn't, until a few minutes ago." Jed gazed up at Leslie and straight into the blazing sun. She was wearing a white visor and red sunglasses that matched her suit, he observed through squinted eyes. He was sorry now that he had left his sunglasses in the van. Shading his eyes with his hand, he paused to think of how to phrase his next question properly.

"I'll give you three guesses," he began, trying to sound confident. "What am I planning to do tomorrow?"

Leslie laughed. "You're going to go windsurfing and you want me to go along and give you some pointers."

"Wrong. Guess again."

"You're going hang gliding and you want me to watch you take off."

"Wrong. Guess again." Jed grinned.

Leslie shook her head. "Surfing?" All the while Leslie was guessing, Jed noticed that she kept her eyes on the ocean. In a way that made his proposal a lot easier to make. At least she couldn't actually *see* him making a fool of himself.

"Wrong," he said. "Three strikes and you're out. No more guesses. I'm going abalone diving."

"Oh, Jed, why didn't you give me another guess? That's what I was going to say next."

"Really?" Jed's mouth dropped open.

"Of course not, silly. I was just kidding. Are you really going abalone diving? I've gone skin diving, but I've never dived for abalone. It sounds like a lot of fun," Leslie admitted.

"Now guess who I've also rented diving equipment for," Jed went on, encouraged by her reply.

"Jacques Cousteau."

"No."

"My brother."

"No."

"Alex."

"Very funny." Jed made a face. "No. Three strikes and you're out again. I rented a whole set of equipment for *you!* Would you like to go with me tomorrow?" He held up one hand. "Hey, don't get me wrong! I understand all about you and Jeff. I'm asking you to go as my diving partner."

"Oh, Jed, that's really nice of you. I'd love to go. Jeff is working tomorrow, but I have the day off."

"Really? You want to go with me?" Jed could hardly believe his luck.

"I just said so, didn't I?" Leslie answered, but she didn't sound annoyed.

"Yeah, I guess you did."

"Have you ever heard of Stillwater Cove?"
Now it was Leslie's turn to ask a question.

Jed shook his head. "No. Why?"

"Well, one of the lifeguards went scuba
diving there last weekend and said that it was
a diver's paradise. The water's real clear and
teeming with all kinds of interesting sea life. If
you don't have a particular place in mind, we
might go there."

As Leslie talked, Jed could hardly get over
the fact that she was so totally receptive to the
idea of going with him anywhere—and she
was even helping to plan their outing. He had
read that Abalone Cove was the best place to
dive for abalone, but what did he care? One
coastal cove was pretty much like the other.
Besides, it wasn't where he went, but with
whom that mattered to him.

"Sure," he replied. "Sounds great. I didn't
have anything definite in mind. Do you know
where that place is?"

"He said it was about forty miles up the
coast."

"We can check it out on a map to make
sure," Jed said.

At that moment, Leslie blew the whistle
hanging around her neck. Jed turned toward
the water and saw what Leslie must have
already spotted: two teenage boys horsing
around and dunking a giggling girl. The boys

looked up, startled, and went back to their water play. But the girl wasn't laughing anymore. She seemed to be struggling.

"Listen, Jed, I'd better go down and break up their little fun before things get out of hand." Leslie sprang from her lifeguard's chair, climbed down the ladder, and jumped onto the sand.

"Maybe tonight we'll work out the details," Jed shouted after her as she started running toward the water's edge.

"I can't tonight. How about over breakfast tomorrow?" Leslie called over her shoulder.

"Sure, great," Jed yelled. But, in truth, it wasn't so great. He kicked the sand several times as he dragged his feet on the way back to the van. Leslie's enthusiasm for their excursion tomorrow had given him the false idea that he was making progress with her. Once again, he had forgotten all about Jeff, but Leslie obviously hadn't. Why did he always have to push things with Leslie just when they seemed to be going so well? When, he wondered, would he learn to be a little more subtle?

As Jed passed the volleyball courts, he halfheartedly waved to Russ, then checked his watch. Thank God it was nearing noon, he thought. When all else failed, he could always take comfort in a Big Beef, Big Fries, and a Big

Gulp. Then **he** remembered that junk food was a no-no, thanks to Pamela. If he planned to stay on his diet, he couldn't stuff his face and drown his disappointments in food the way he used to.

He walked past a row of parked cars until he reached his van. As he backed out of the space, the car seemed to be in control of itself. It wanted to turn the corner and head straight up the street to Big Boy. The moment was a real test of willpower for Jed. He struggled with the big steering wheel for several minutes, but at last he got the better of it. He turned north on Surfrider and headed back to the house, where he could fix himself a tuna-salad sandwich.

Chapter 9

After not blowing his diet at Big Boy, Jed didn't feel quite so low. In fact, he was quite proud of himself. Although it had been a close call, he had stuck to his resolution. And now that he thought about it, he didn't feel so bad about how things had gone with Leslie, either. She hadn't thought twice before she'd said she'd love to go diving with him. And why should he care if she was going out with Jeff tonight? She was spending the whole day with him, not Jeff, tomorrow, wasn't she? That thought really lifted his spirits. Then why was he moping around in his room feeling sorry for himself?

With the sun up and shining brightly since early this morning, it was a perfect day, Jed decided, to try out his snorkeling equipment.

In the spring, before coming down to Marina Bay, he had bought the full black wet suit from an over-the-hill surfer at a garage sale. He had tried it on then, but, now, five months later, he wasn't really sure how it would fit. It wouldn't hurt to test out the suit and all the other equipment before taking any deep-sea dives.

With a sudden burst of energy, Jed jumped up from his bed and stripped down to his undershorts and socks. Then he dragged the wet suit and everything else out of the closet. That was the easy part. Putting everything on, Jed soon discovered, posed some unexpected problems. He got the booties on over his socks, all right. He had remembered that they went on first. But getting the heavy rubber one-piece suit on over the booties was easier said than done. He struggled to pull it over his ankles, but when rubber hit rubber, nothing budged. He tugged and tugged until he was sweating from the effort. Finally, he worked the legs up over the booties, but by then his skin was so wet that the suit stuck to it. He squirmed and wriggled until he pulled the suit over his thick legs and chunky middle, all the while feeling like an old lady getting into her girdle. At last he had the suit on, except for the arms.

But before going any further, he needed a rest. He sat down on the bed again, took a deep breath, and then tried to stuff one arm into the sleeve. It wouldn't slide through. What was wrong? Jed wondered. Had his arms gotten fatter in five months? Finally he realized that he had to ease his arms into the sleeves, the way he had put on the rest of the suit. Then he picked up the hood, face mask, snorkel, and fins from the floor, leaving the weight belt and gloves for last.

Now to stand up with an extra fifteen pounds hugging his hips and with fins on his feet. That was the tricky part. On Jed's first try, the weight of the belt forced him back on the bed again. The next time he rocked back and forth on the bed first, then shot himself forward to pick up momentum. He successfully propelled himself upright, but when he bent over to pick up the gloves, he almost fell over his funny-looking feet.

Finally Jed was standing on his own two fins. He clumped over to the full-length mirror on the inside of his closet door to see how he looked completely suited up. He was pleased with the image before him. The snug-fitting, all-black suit did make him appear a little thinner. Of course, he'd have a better idea when the back, which he couldn't close himself, was zipped up.

He headed downstairs to see if anyone was home to help him with the zipper. But walking web-footed with fifteen pounds around his middle down a flight of stairs was no mean feat. The fins were too long for the stairs, and judging distance with a face mask on didn't make the task of getting down them any easier. Jed ended up sidestepping down, all the while wondering why he had been so stupid as to put everything on before coming downstairs in the first place. When he reached the hallway, he looked around as best he could to see if anyone was downstairs. No luck. He waddled out on the deck, hoping to find either Pamela or Tracy. As he slid open the glass door and awkwardly stomped outside, he considered sleeping on the beach in the suit. No matter how uncomfortable it would be to wear overnight, it had to be better than having to struggle into it again tomorrow.

Jed saw a pair of shapely legs out on the lounger that could belong to either one of his female housemates. But when Jed also saw a head of wild, dark hair cascading over the back of the lounger, he immediately recognized Tracy sunning herself on the deck.

"Tracy, could you do me a favor?" he asked in a muffled voice under his face mask.

"Aah," Tracy squealed, shielding her face with her hands as Jed duck-walked a step closer. "I'm being attacked by the creature from the Black Lagoon."

Jed flipped up his face mask. "Don't be scared. It's me, Jed."

"Well, what do you know. You had me fooled there for a second," Tracy snickered. "You certainly have a flair for dressing. What's the occasion? Does your date have a thing for deep-sea divers?"

"Well, sort of," Jeff admitted. "I'm going abalone diving with Leslie tomorrow."

Tracy raised an eyebrow. "Leslie, huh? Jeff must be working tomorrow. And what he doesn't know, won't hurt him." Tracy winked.

"It's nothing like that, Tracy," Jed said quickly—too quickly. "Leslie and I have an understanding. We have a completely platonic relationship." For the time being, anyway, Jed added to himself.

"I hope so. I've heard Jeff has a real jealous streak."

"Well, I'm not going to worry about it. There's nothing between Leslie and me for him to get all worked up about," Jeff said. All the same, he was glad when Tracy changed the subject. "Aren't you going to get a little overheated in that suit if you're not going diving until tomorrow?"

"Oh, I'm on my way to the water to test out my equipment," Jed told her, feeling ridiculous. "I just need someone to zip up the back for me."

"Turn around," Tracy said, reaching up for the zipper. It went up without a struggle. "There, darling," Tracy teased. "Now turn around again and let me see how you look." Jed flipped down his mask and struck a macho deep sea diver pose. "Marvelous, darling," she drawled approvingly.

"Thanks, Tracy," Jed said, his voice muffled.

"What?"

He flipped up the mask. "I said, thanks, Tracy. By the way, where's Fury?"

"Need you ask? I'm a surf widow again today." She sighed. "It's hard on a girl, sharing her boyfriend with the surf. If you see him out there, send him my regards," Tracy said.

"Sure thing. Thanks again." Then Jed tee-tered off the deck and onto the sand.

As soon as he began to duck-foot across it, he recognized how much easier it would be to walk without webbed feet. But the sun was right above him, so the sand would be too hot for him to walk on barefoot. Unless he wanted scorched soles, he had no choice now but to cross the beach wearing his fins.

With the weight belt around his waist, the going was slow. Jed felt like he was plodding across the Sahara Desert. He didn't have to worry about getting sunburned, since he was wearing his wet suit, but the black neoprene didn't breathe, and absorbed the strong rays of the afternoon sun.

By the time he reached the wet, packed sand where the waddling was a little easier, Jed couldn't wait to get into the water. But when he reached the edge of the surf, he hit himself on the forehead with one gloved hand. How dumb could he get? It had just occurred to him that he could have left his weight belt at the house instead of weighting himself down as he trudged across the beach. He immediately dropped the belt at the water's edge. Then he waded into the water and dived under an oncoming wave, popping up again on the other side. He swam out until he reached a kelp bed, where the water was warmer and less turbulent.

Water trickled into his suit, instantly cooling off his body. Jed knew that a little water inside the suit was to be expected. The used wet suit and diving accessories passed the test with flying colors, and Jed felt comfortable wearing them in the water. Best of all, he could experience the same wonderful feeling of weightlessness he had felt when he had gone hang gliding.

Accustomed now to the feel of his full wet suit and the temperature of the surf, Jed lowered his face mask into the water and concentrated on controlling his breathing. He hoped to have his underwater breathing technique down before tomorrow so he could review it with Leslie. It wouldn't, he realized, hurt his cause if she were impressed by his lecture.

As soon as Jed was breathing regularly through his snorkel, he became acutely aware of the beauty and color of the three-dimensional aquatic world around him. Tiny, iridescent fish darted playfully through and around his fingers, distracting him from his equipment check. He snorkeled slowly around the kelp bed, his face mask coming so close to a lobster that he could see its feelers twitch. Next, a passing school of anchovies clouded the water, cutting off the sunlight for a moment.

He was so fascinated by the underwater world swimming right by him that he almost didn't notice the sea lion that stopped just inches from his face mask. In his sleek black wet suit, Jed felt among friends. The sea lion wriggled its whiskers at him and seemed to consider Jed one of its own, too.

As Jed practiced breathing through his snorkel, taking in fresh air from above and the magic of the sea world from below, he couldn't remember when he had felt more relaxed and removed from all the pressures and troubles of the dry world. The problems he had been having with girls all summer and the importance of making a good impression on Leslie tomorrow seemed the furthest things from his mind.

But just when he thought he could float mindlessly on water forever, a shiver ran through his body. He had been in the water quite a long time. He suddenly felt chilled and decided he should head back in. His fins knifed the water and he swiftly reached shore. He took off his fins and walked over the beach, this time actually enjoying the warmth of the sand on the soles of his feet.

When Jed finally reached the Stevens's house, he dropped his gear on the redwood deck and spent a few minutes struggling to open the zipper in the back of the suit. Getting out of the suit now that it was wet and had stretched a little was a snap compared to how difficult it had been to get into it.

Wearing only his damp briefs, he made a beeline to the bathroom, wrapped a towel around his waist, and headed to the kitchen.

He hadn't felt hungry in the water, but now he felt as if he could eat a horse. He opened the refrigerator and took out some assorted cold cuts and mayonnaise. Then he found a whole loaf of French bread in the bread drawer, sliced it in half and went to work making himself a foot-long submarine sandwich. Finally, he went in search of some dessert.

Rummaging around in the cupboards for anything sweet, he found four slightly stale doughnuts in a pink bakery box. As far as Jed was concerned they were perfectly edible. He took the pastries in one hand and his sandwich in the other and carried them over to the dining-room table.

In his ravenous state, Jed completely forgot that he had just started a major diet. He took a bite of his oversized sandwich, then decided he couldn't wait until he finished all of it before trying a doughnut. He opened the box only to be confronted by a new dilemma: which of the four tasty doughnuts to eat first.

"Jed Mason, *what* are you eating?" Pamela cried, suddenly stepping into the dining room through the sliding glass door. Russ was right behind her. They were both in their bathing suits and carrying towels, obviously having spent the afternoon at Seahorse Shores Beach.

Ignoring Pamela, Jed took a bite out of the doughnut.

"Really, Jed, you shouldn't be eating that. Doughnuts are the worst thing for you. They're fried in grease," Pamela pointed out.

"I'm starving," Jed pleaded, looking from Pamela to Russ, who appeared to be trying hard not to laugh.

"Then eat a piece of fruit," Pamela suggested.

Jed reluctantly put the doughnut back in the box and picked up his sandwich.

"*Now* what are you eating?" Pamela inquired, raising her eyebrows.

"What does it look like? It's a sandwich." Jed was really getting annoyed now. Why wouldn't the two of them just go away and leave him to stuff his face in peace.

"It's a sandwich for an elephant. That's three times as much bread as you should be eating. Now put it down," Pamela admonished him.

"I'm an elephant. Thanks, Jed," Russ said, pretending his arm was an elephant's trunk and swooping up the hero sandwich just as Jed put it back on his plate.

"How come Russ can eat it and I can't?" Jed complained.

"When you're Russ's size, you can eat a sandwich that size," Pamela said, beaming lovingly at Russ. Obviously pleased by the compliment, Russ raised the long hero above his head as if it were a dumbbell.

One look at the ideal couple was all it took to get Jed back on track. He thought of how one day Leslie would smile like that at him, and he walked straight into the kitchen to grab an apple from the fruit bowl.

"That's better," Pamela said when Jed came back into the dining room. "Now let's get this nasty stuff out of the house. Then you won't be tempted to eat it." She picked up the pink box and headed into the kitchen. "Say good-bye to your doughnuts," she said triumphantly as she dumped them into the trash can.

"Good-bye doughnuts," Jed called to them. *And hello, Leslie*, he added as he took another bite of his apple.

Chapter 10

On Sunday afternoon, when Jed got into his wet suit again, it wasn't quite the ordeal it had been the day before. And to Jed's delight, Leslie, not Tracy, zipped up the back for him. Now they were both suited up and perched on the rocks at Stillwater Cove, ready to make their entry.

Over breakfast on the deck, as Leslie had suggested, they had discussed how to get there. In the morning, it had looked as if the day was shaping up into another one of those picture-postcard sunny Southern California days, so they had decided to cruise up the coast in Leslie's open jeep. The drive was forty miles up the scenic coast.

When they had gotten all their gear together

and were ready to leave, Leslie had wanted to drive, and Jed had no objections. As they sped up the coast, he'd been free to chatter away about diving and to review with Leslie how to breathe and what to look for underwater, and how long to stay down. So enthralled had Jed been with his own lecture and the fact that he'd been sitting right next to Leslie the whole ride, that it never once crossed his mind that she had been out with Jeff the night before. He had gotten the impression from the way Leslie listened that her thoughts had been 100 percent with him as he talked.

And now, after they had positioned their face masks, Jed waited for a tidal surge to take them out over the rocks. With Leslie beside him, the thrill of taking their first dive together was now at hand. When the tide rushed in, Jed motioned to her to throw in the float and jump.

Jed hit the ocean and Leslie followed him into the water with a big splash. Then they began to swim, the mesh game bag hanging from around Jed's neck filtering the water after them.

Once they were out beyond the rocks, they neared a kelp bed and floated on the surface of the ocean facedown, breathing with the aid of their snorkels. They propelled themselves through the water with their fins until Jed spotted what he thought was an abalone ten feet below. He pointed it out to Leslie, then motioned to her to take some deep breaths in preparation for a dive. He took her hand and they dived straight down. They swam among the sea creatures for a few minutes: spiny purple urchins, red starfish, and a stingray lying still and flat on the sandy bottom. As their flippers made ripples through the water, the disturbed ray swam off.

Jed quickly looked around and spotted some likely-looking abalone shapes clinging to some nearby rocks. With sea sponges, sea anemones, moss, and algae growing on their shells, they were well camouflaged. At first it was hard for him to distinguish them from the rocks. Only when his face mask was actually touching an abalone shell was Jed sure he had come upon an abalone colony.

He took out his ab iron from its sheath and slipped the rope tied to one end around his wrist. Then he tried to pry an abalone off a rock. On his first attempt, he moved too slowly. The creature reacted to Jed's slight touch and, using its foot like a plumber's helper, seized more tightly onto the rock. On his second try Jed moved more swiftly and, catching an abalone off guard, flipped it easily off the rock with his ab iron. He opened his mesh bag, dropped it in, and motioned to Leslie to surface.

After depositing their first abalone in the rubber float above them, they went down again—three more times, in fact. Now that Jed knew where to look for them, bagging the next three sea creatures was almost as easy as a trip to the supermarket. In fact, after the fourth dive, Jed was growing a little bored with the process. The hardest part was holding your breath as long as it took to dive down, pry the abalone loose from the rock surface, and come up again. Even Leslie, Jed noticed, had mastered the diving skills.

After they had surfaced and stored their fourth abalone inside the float, Jed slipped the rope attached to his ab iron around Leslie's wrist and suggested, "Why don't you get the last one? Prying the abalone loose is pretty easy. Just insert the iron between the shell and the rock and you've got it made."

"I'm sure I can do it. I've been watching you. Let's go," Leslie exclaimed, obviously excited by the prospect of catching her own dinner.

In her eagerness, she upended herself in the water and went down just ahead of Jed. He followed her for about ten feet, to the spot where he had collected the other four hard-shelled snails. There Leslie began to poke in some crevices with the iron.

She tapped something hard with the end of the pry bar, but unlike the fairly immobile game Jed had bagged, it had eyes and many teeth that snapped at the rope between the ab iron and her wrist as it opened its jaw. The next thing Jed saw it had clamped its jagged teeth into the piece of rope. Leslie drew back in horror, but the thing held on. Inadvertently she dragged the three-foot-long, dragonlike sea serpent out of its hiding place and along with her as she frantically kicked her flippers to get away from it.

Jed motioned to her to shake the ab iron off her wrist, but Leslie couldn't understand his gesture. The dark green, speckled, snakelike fish with a huge head and two rows of sharp teeth trailed along with her as she propelled herself upward. Just as Leslie was about to surface, the rope slipped off her wrist by itself.

Jed watched the ab iron, with the moray eel's teeth still sunk in the rope and the long, slippery body wriggling after, drift to the bottom of the ocean. Unconcerned about the iron, he turned his attention to Leslie.

She had already surfaced, and Jed popped out of the water right next to her. But as soon as he was about to say something to calm her down, she started swimming off toward shore. When she reached the spot where they had entered the water, she scurried up onto the rocks, with Jed right behind her. It cost him a lot of energy to keep up with a lifeguard.

Leslie pulled off her mask and hood, sat down on the rocks, and started to shake. Jed flung off his own mask and threw his arms around her.

"Everything's okay, Leslie," he said softly, stroking her hair. "You just disturbed a moray eel in its habitat, that's all."

"You mean it disturbed *me*," Leslie replied, sniffling.

"Me, too," Jed admitted. "Morays are pretty ugly. But they're usually passive. I think this one mistook the rope for its next meal. They don't usually attack humans," he assured her, his arms still wrapped tightly around her cold body.

Jed sat that way until Leslie stopped shaking and he was sure that she had completely calmed down. Then without another word, they helped each other out of their skin diving equipment and stretched out on the rock to dry off. Before long they had both fallen asleep in the warm, soothing sun.

When Jed awoke about an hour later, he found Leslie sitting up, apparently recovered from her fright.

"Don't you think we should get the abalone out of the water?" she asked anxiously.

Jed nodded. "You're right. In all the excitement, I forgot all about them. We need to clean them and get them in the ice chest before they spoil. I'll go back and get the float out of the water," he offered.

"And I'll get the ice chest out of the jeep," Leslie said.

A few minutes later, they met near the rest rooms at the long metal sink especially designed for cleaning abalone. Jed placed them in the sink.

"I'll clean one first, and you can do the next one," he said, picking up an abalone. He took a sharp knife and slipped it as far as he could between the shell and the flesh and pressed down on the handle of the knife until the flesh tore away from its attachment point.

"Now here's the tricky part," Jed explained. He put the knife down on the connecting worktable and slipped his free hand under the slippery muscle. "If I do this right, I should be able to separate the edible part from the part you throw away." He pulled the muscle out of the shell in one quick upward jerk. "There, I did it," he said. "Now it's your turn."

Leslie, always a quick learner, was equally successful. Soon they had all the abalone ready for the next step, the cutting and slicing. Jed trimmed away the dark outer, tough parts on the table and sliced the remaining muscle into abalone steaks.

"Now comes the fun part," Jed announced. "The pounding." He took some plastic bags from the ice chest and slipped the steaks into them, then took out a mallet and went to work. When he had beaten a couple of steaks to a pulp, he gave Leslie a turn. Between the two of them, they finished the preparations just as the sun started dropping in the sky.

"I'm getting a little cold," Leslie said.

"We finished just in time," Jed replied. "Let's pack up."

"Why don't we stop for dinner on the way home? I know a great fish restaurant right on the coast. It's really cheap and not too fancy. It's also not too far from here," Leslie said as they pulled out on the highway.

"Sounds great. I'm starving," Jed admitted. His breakfast had been another diet special and, in the excitement of being with Leslie all day, he had skipped lunch altogether. Could he live on love alone?

But after Leslie had driven about ten miles down the coast and they were seated next to a window at the Tides Inn, Jed decided to forget about his diet for one meal.

"I wonder how they prepare their abalone here," he mused as he scanned the menu.

"How *do* you prepare abalone?" Leslie asked.

"Well, first you dip the steaks in salted, beaten eggs, then roll them in bread crumbs, and fry them. That's all there is to it," Jed explained, hoping he sounded like an abalone expert.

A waiter came over to their table and hovered over them.

Leslie nodded. "Great, we can make them one night at home. But maybe we'd better concentrate on what we're going to have tonight," she added, glancing up at the patient waiter.

"I'll have the fried oysters with french fries," Jed told the waiter.

"I thought you were on a diet," Leslie reminded him with a grin.

Jed looked up at the waiter again. "Make that the grilled swordfish with a salad and a Diet Coke."

"And I'll have the fried oysters with french fries and a regular Coke." The minute the waiter walked away, she said, "You know, Jed, I can't remember when I've had a more exhilarating time."

After that, it really didn't matter what Jed had ordered for dinner. "Me, too," Jed gulped. But he couldn't help wondering if that included the times Leslie had spent with Jeff.

"I have to admit," Leslie went on, "between teaching you how to windsurf, watching you hang glide, and now, going diving, we've had a lot of fun together this summer. I'm glad we're such good friends."

"Me, too," Jed said again. He was willing to wait for the day when they'd be more than friends. When that day came, however, he hoped he could handle it better than he was dealing with this conversation. It was hard enough for him just to speak without getting tongue-tied sitting opposite Leslie. She was so attractive and put together he could hardly get his words out.

He was glad when their waiter interrupted them and set their food before them. But all during dinner, as Leslie devoured her fried oysters and french fries, he still couldn't take his eyes off her and hardly touched his food. Maybe he *could* live on love alone, he decided.

The soft light of dusk brushed across her face and highlighted her sun-bleached hair and glowing skin. After Leslie had finished her dinner, she seemed, Jed noticed, to have eyes only for the changing evening sky just outside their window. He didn't mind so much that she wasn't looking at him now. While she stared out the window, he could gaze longingly at her.

By the time Leslie had polished off her lemon meringue pie—and Jed, who had restrained himself, his coffee—it was dark outside. Although Leslie insisted that they go Dutch treat, Jed wouldn't hear of it.

"Thanks for a terrific day and a lovely

dinner," Leslie said, as Jed opened the door on the driver's side of the jeep for her. As they drove along the water on their way back home, Jed couldn't get over how perfectly the whole day had gone.

Except for Leslie's scare with the moray eel, she had obviously loved everything about the abalone diving adventure. And he loved, well . . . He couldn't stop himself now from putting his arm on the back of her seat and inching it around her shoulder.

"Don't, Jed," Leslie said immediately. "Don't confuse things. We have an agreement, right?"

"Sorry, Leslie. I guess I got carried away," he replied, reminding himself that he had promised not to push things.

Suddenly there was a loud bang and Jed saw Leslie struggling with the wheel as she tried to steer the car over onto the shoulder of the road.

"I think you've got a flat," Jed announced as the jeep came to a stop on the side of the road.

"Oh, no," Leslie groaned. "Just our luck. I've never had a flat in the jeep before. I don't even know how to change a tire," she lamented.

"No problem. I'll teach you. Where's your manual?" Jed asked.

"In the glove compartment." She flicked on the interior light so that Jed could read the

little instruction book. "It looks pretty standard," Jed said after a quick glance. "You'll
need your jack and a flashlight."

Leslie reached under her seat and pulled
out a tool kit. "The flashlight's in the glove
compartment."

Jed sat back. "Okay, here's what I want you
to do."

Leslie looked at him in surprise. "Aren't *you*
going to change it?" she asked, sounding
puzzled.

"What good will that do? You should change
it so if this happens again you'll know what to
do. I'll hold the flashlight and coach you
through it, okay?" He got out of the jeep and
walked around to where the spare tire was
mounted on the back. Leslie trailed behind.

"Okay. The first thing you do is remove the
spare tire from its bracket with the lug
wrench." Leslie did as Jed had directed and
handed the spare tire to Jed. He rolled it
around to the flat in front.

"Now loosen the wheel nuts with the lug
wrench," he instructed, shining the flashlight
on the wheel.

"Okay, wheel nuts loosened. What's next?"
Leslie asked. "Hey, Jed, this is kind of fun. Jeff
never lets me help when he has to change a
flat. All he does is groan and complain and
make me feel sorry for him."

"Well, I'm not feeling sorry for you," Jed replied, knowing he sounded as deflated as Leslie's tire. "Now let's concentrate on what we're doing here."

"I'm sorry, Jed. I shouldn't have brought Jeff up," Leslie apologized.

"Just forget it," Jed answered stiffly. "Now where were we? Oh, yeah. Now you attach the jack to the frame. There should be a slot for the jack under there."

"I've found it," Leslie said quickly.

"Good. Now loosen the wheel nuts and jack up the car with the lever."

As Leslie cranked up the front of the car, then changed the tire as Jed instructed, he was amazed at how well she handled the tools. *There wasn't anything that girl couldn't do. Except fall for me,* he added dejectedly.

"That's all there is to it?" Leslie asked after she and Jed were once again seated in the jeep.

"That's it," he replied. "You've changed a tire all by yourself. There's nothing to it."

"I couldn't have done it without your help, Jed," Leslie said, her big eyes looking very blue, even in the darkness.

She started the engine, flipped on the headlights and directional signal, and waited for the traffic to clear. "I don't plan to have another flat unless you're in the car with me," she joked as she pulled back onto the road.

"I hope I am," Jed replied. "But some things you can't plan." Then he put his arm around Leslie's shoulder again.

He could feel her tense up, and he was sure she was going to ask him to remove it. But Leslie said only, "I guess you're right. Some things you just can't plan. You know, Jed, you're really a one-of-a-kind type guy." He could feel her relax a bit into the crook of his arm.

Chapter 11

When Jed came downstairs dressed for another Monday morning of baby-sitting Alex at the beach, he wasn't surprised to find Leslie still running around the house. To begin with, they had gotten home late last night, and by the time they had hosed down both their gear and themselves and stored the abalone steaks in the freezer, it was almost one o'clock. But Jed was amazed to see Leslie wearing another sundress. His heart sank. Jeff again.

"You look really nice today," he said, hesitating a little. Even if she *was* wearing a dress for Jeff's benefit, there was no law that said he couldn't appreciate how pretty she looked.

"Thanks," Leslie replied, sounding somewhat distracted. "Have you seen my beach bag?"

"I think it's in the living room. Can I make you some breakfast?" Jed offered as Leslie gathered up her things for the day.

"Don't have time," she answered. "I overslept. Now Jeff's going to give it to me for being late. Whoops, I mean, I've got to go." She snatched her red beach bag from the coffee table in the living room. Suddenly she stopped and quickly added, "But I don't care. It was worth it. I had a wonderful time yesterday."

"Yeah, me, too," Jed said. "Maybe I'll see you on the beach today. I have to come into town anyway to return your gear." He was glad that he had a legitimate excuse for going into Marina Bay. He didn't want to let the whole day go by without seeing Leslie. It had been torture enough to walk her to her room last night and just say good night. Although she had rested her head against his arm as they drove home, she had made it clear that she didn't want Jed to try anything more. But he had gone to bed happy that Leslie had let his arm be around her at all.

"Great. See you later," she said and flew out of the house.

Jed, too, was running late. He had only fifteen minutes left before he'd have to pick up

Alex. Nevertheless, he took enough time to fix himself a bowl of cold cereal and milk. He purposely packed a light lunch so he wouldn't be tempted to grab some fattening food on fast-food row. Pamela would be proud of him.

"I have a surprise for you," Jed told Alex as soon as the little kid was belted in and they were on their way into town.

"Yippee! A surprise! I love surprises! I want to know what it is now," Alex insisted.

"If I tell you now, it won't be a surprise," Jed pointed out.

"I want to know *now*! I want to—"

"Okay, okay, Alex. I'll tell you. We're spending the day on Marina Bay Beach instead of Seahorse Shores."

"That's not a surprise. I hate that surprise. I don't want to go to that beach. I like my beach better," Alex whined, sulking all too predictably.

"But I thought you'd *like* going to a different beach for a change. Listen, I heard the sand is better for making sand castles at Marina Bay Beach."

"Really?" Alex asked, his eyes wide.

"Yep. It's true."

Alex got very quiet, and Jed knew he had won this round. Alex was a smart kid, but Jed was no match for him. Even if he hadn't outwitted Alex, however, he would have taken the little carrottop by the hair and dragged him kicking and screaming to Marina Bay Beach. No way was he not going to be near Leslie.

Jed drove down Surfrider, past all the beach-front stores where the pre-teen crowd hung out, the surfer hangout, and T-shirts for Two, where Tracy worked during the day. Taking in the passing scene kept seven-year-old Alex occupied until Jed turned up Windward Way and into the Wilderness Supply Shop parking lot.

"Where are we going? I thought we were going to the beach!" Alex wailed.

"We are," Jed replied easily. "I just have to return something."

"I want to go *now*," Alex insisted.

"This will just take a minute. Come on," Jed coaxed, unbelting Alex and helping the little boy out of his seat.

As it turned out, it took Jed forty-five minutes—five to return the rented scuba gear, and forty for Alex to pick out an inflatable water toy. Jed couldn't get Alex to settle for an inexpensive water ring. Instead, he made Alex happy and himself ten dollars poorer with the purchase of a Gumby blow-up raft that was twice the size of Alex. In fact, it was bigger than Jed.

Of course it was Jed, not Alex, who ended

up dragging the ridiculously oversized float across the beach. Alex insisted that all he could possibly carry was his pail and shovel. With towels tucked under his arm, the ice chest in one hand, and the green Gumby in the other, Jed could hardly see where he was going. The inflated thing was even too large to hold under one arm. Its squared-off green head kept popping up into Jed's face, obscuring his vision. The next thing he knew, Jed bumped into someone very tall and solid.

"Hey, watch where you're going!"

"Sorry," Jed mumbled, shifting the blow-up raft aside and finding himself looking straight into Jeff's angry face.

"Oh, it's *you*," Jeff said, scowling. "What a coincidence. You're just the person I wanted to run into today."

"Well, you certainly did," Jed said, hoping that a little humor might lighten up the situation.

"Cut the comedy, pal. I'm in no mood for jokes from you."

Jed got the message. A thousand clowns standing on their heads couldn't get Jeff to crack a smile right now, he realized. And Jed had a pretty good idea why Jeff was out looking for him.

"What kind of guy are you, anyway?" Jeff asked, crossing his well-muscled arms across his chest. "First you take out Leslie—*my girl*—and keep her out till all hours of the night so she's late to work. Then, like a wimp, you get her to fix her own flat tire. You know what I'd like to do right now?" Jed didn't think he should venture a guess. "I'd like to flatten your head so it looks like that big green plastic buddy of yours."

"Don't you dare hurt my baby-sitter," Alex piped up.

"Shut up, kid," Jeff snapped.

"What if I don't want to?" The little boy clenched his fists.

"Alex, you stay out of this. I can fight my own battles," Jed said. If only he had started his weight-training program a little earlier in the summer so he could make good on his words! If he were in better shape, he wouldn't have to let Jeff get away with calling him a wimp. Let Jeff start something a few weeks from now, Jed fumed, and he'd show him a thing or two.

"I'm going to give you one, and only one, warning," Jeff continued, not seeming the least bit threatened by Jed and his sidekick. "Stay away from Leslie."

"What if I don't want to?" Jed shot back, borrowing a line from Alex. "Besides, it would be a little difficult for me to do, since we live in the same house."

"Don't get smart," Jeff growled. "You know what I mean."

"No, I don't know what you mean," Jed said, holding his ground as well as the towels, the ice chest, and Gumby. "There's absolutely nothing between Leslie and me. You can ask her yourself. We just went out diving for the day, that's all."

"And got home after midnight? That's a long time to spend underwater."

Jed's mouth dropped open. "How do you know what time we got home? What did you do, follow us?"

"No, wise-ass. I asked Leslie why she was late this morning, and she told me all about your day *and* the flat tire she had to fix. A real man wouldn't let a girl do work like that!"

Jed let that remark pass. He'd only be wasting his breath trying to explain to macho Jeff that he had wanted Leslie to learn how to change a tire by herself. "Listen, Jeff, Leslie and I are just friends. Do you think she would have told you about yesterday if there was anything more between us?" Jed knew, despite Jeff's warning, that he would see Leslie again. But he wanted to set the record straight first.

"I want to go in the water with Gumby," Alex demanded.

For once Jed was more than glad to give in to him. "I've got to go, Jeff," he said with a shrug. "Alex is getting antsy." He turned away and started walking across the sand. Alex strutted behind him, beating a marching rhythm on his pail. Jed expected Jeff to yell something after them, but he didn't.

When they had made it a good distance away, Jed checked to see if the dark-haired head lifeguard was following him. To his relief, Jed sighted Jeff storming off in the other direction.

"The next time that guy starts up with me, this is what I'm going to do to him," Jed told Alex with a grin. He set down the towels and ice chest. "I'm going to flatten him." Jed held Gumby by the arm, gave him a right to his jaw, and let go of the toy. Alex laughed as Gumby landed on his back in the sand, its round black eyes staring up at them. The big red mouth was still smiling. "Round one goes to the Berkeley man in the blue trunks," Jed announced, raising his arms above his head like a boxing champ.

By the time he and Alex reached the water's edge, Jed was unusually happy to play with the kid. He liked the way the little guy had stood up for him to Jeff. Jed dropped everything he had been carrying onto the sand. Alex slipped out of his water sandals and took off toward the water. "Last one in is a rotten egg," he shouted when he had a sufficient lead.

Jed kicked off his sneakers, grabbed Gumby by the arm, and ran after Alex.

"You're a rotten egg. You're a rotten egg," the redheaded boy chanted as Jed entered the water with a huge splash.

After an hour or so of water play, Jed noticed that Alex was shivering. "How about some lunch, pal?" he asked.

"Only if Gumby is hungry," Alex replied.

"Are you hungry, Gumby?" Jed asked the big toy. He made Gumby's head nod yes.

"Lunchtime," Jed called out as he headed back to the beach.

Just as he was about to wrap a brightly colored towel around Alex, Leslie, wearing the sundress over her bathing suit, strolled up.

"I thought I spotted Alex's red hair from the tower," she said, smiling. "Can I join you guys for a while? I'm on my lunch break."

"Sure," Jed and Alex replied at the same time. Jed started to dry off the squirming little boy.

"Here, let me do that," Leslie offered. She set her beach bag down in the sand and gently started to rub Alex's wet head. He nuzzled into the towel like a cat being scratched behind the ears.

Before Jed had a chance to say anything, Alex asked, "Why don't you have lunch with us, Leslie?"

Leslie glanced at Jed. "Sure, thanks. But I'm not really all that hungry. I'll tell you what. After Alex eats up all his lunch like a good boy, why don't we walk up to the soda shop? I'll buy you an ice-cream cone."

Alex looked up at Leslie with love in his eyes. *Join the long line of smitten admirers, Alex,* Jed grimaced to himself.

"If I eat up all *my* lunch like a good boy, what will *I* get?" Jed couldn't resist.

"What would you want?" she flirted back.

Jed didn't answer, but he was glad that he hadn't had a chance to bring his confrontation with Jeff into the conversation. With Leslie being so friendly, there was no need for him to get her thinking about her boyfriend again.

After Jed and Alex had finished their lunch, Leslie snatched up her bag and said, "Okay, Alex, time for ice cream!"

Jed let the air out of Gumby and helped Alex put on his shoes. Then they all headed up the beach toward the Flotsam and Jetsamwich Shop. Alex, without being asked, took Leslie's hand. Now Jed felt more deflated than Gumby. He never thought he'd be jealous of a seven-year-old, but he couldn't help wishing Leslie had taken *his* hand instead of Alex's. *How would it feel to hold her hand?* Jed asked himself as he looked on with envy.

Later, after Leslie had bought Alex and

herself cones—Jed had resisted temptation once again—they all walked over to the volleyball courts to watch Russ play.

"Okay, you can have some," Leslie teased when she noticed Jed's eyes on her ice cream.

"Just a taste," Jed assured her, taking the cone from Leslie's hand.

Of course eagle-eyed Pamela showed up at that very moment. "Now, now, Jed, that's no way to stay on a diet. It's a good thing I come along every now and then to keep you honest."

"It's Leslie's cone," Jed said defensively, handing the rapidly melting treat right back to her as if it were a hot potato. Just his luck, he thought, that Pamela had caught him eating ice cream instead of carrot sticks.

Fortunately, Russ appeared with a volleyball under his arm. "Don't make any plans for tonight," he told them. "After dinner, we're having our first volleyball workout on the beach in front of the house." He turned toward his sister. "And don't you go and tell the enemy what we're up to."

"I wouldn't dream of doing that," Leslie assured Russ sweetly.

Suddenly, Alex tugged at Jed's trunks. He was looking up at him with a chocolate mustache above his lip and tears in his eyes. Jed spotted two melted scoops of rocky road ice cream lying in the sand.

"Oh, that's too bad," Jed said sympathetically. "Come on, we'll play some volleyball." Jed stooped to pick up the ball Russ had put down next to the volleyball stanchion and started a game of catch with Alex. In no time at all, the redheaded kid had forgotten all about his ice cream. He was his happy self again as he and Jed tossed the ball back and forth.

"I'd better get back to work," Leslie called to Jed, interrupting their game.

Russ, who had been talking with Pamela, came over and took back the ball to resume his two-man game with Chris. Alex didn't complain. He was delighted with the chance to watch the experts play.

"Thanks for helping me out with Alex," Jed told Leslie.

"No sweat. It was fun." Leslie pushed back the sunglasses on her head. "You know, Jed, I was really impressed with the way you handled Alex just now. Not many guys know how to take care of kids. And not many girls are as good with kids as you, either. I probably would have taken the easy way out and offered to buy Alex another ice cream. But you had the patience to try another approach."

"Hey, Leslie, don't be modest. You're not so bad with Alex yourself. Say, maybe, if . . ." Jed was about to ask Leslie if she was going to be around the house tonight to watch everyone practice, but he quickly bit his tongue. He didn't want to hear her answer. Instead he said, "Maybe, if you want to, we could pool our baby-sitting talents and do this again sometime."

"Sure, Jed. I'll see you later. 'Bye, Alex," Leslie said, tousling the little boy's tufts of red hair.

"Bend down," Alex ordered Leslie. She obligingly lowered herself to Alex's height and he planted a kiss on her cheek. "'Bye, Leslie. Thanks for the ice-cream cone."

"Oh, Alex, that was sweet," Leslie squealed, giving him a kiss on the cheek.

As Jed watched the whole, mushy scene in amazement, he felt so jealous of Alex that he wanted to kill the kid.

Chapter 12

After Alex had succeeded where Jed had failed so far, in completely winning Leslie's heart, Jed had had enough of the two-faced kid. By the time they had walked back to their spot on the beach, Jed was delighted that it was time to take his little Romeo home. He quickly gathered up their belongings and started across the sand. This time he made Alex carry the deflated Gumby all the way back to the van.

After Jed had dropped off Alex and his toys, he knew exactly what he wanted to do until the volleyball workout. He marched straight up to his room and got out some toys of his own—Russ's weights. He worked on strengthening one arm, then the other, for almost an hour. As he huffed and puffed, he was tempted to quit several times, but the memory of Jeff's insults kept him going. The next time the brawny lifeguard started up with him, he'd show him what kind of man he was, Jed vowed. But even with Jeff's taunts to egg him on, Jed eventually grew tired—and hungry. He put the weights away, took a quick shower, and changed into a fresh pair of army shorts and a white T-shirt. Then he headed downstairs to make himself something to eat.

Jed remembered that Pamela had said that a growing boy couldn't live on rabbit food alone. So he made himself a hamburger and a big salad and took a Diet Coke out of the fridge. Just as he set a bottle of ketchup and his dinner down on the table, Jed was delighted to see Pamela walking into the dining room.

If it had come as a shock to him that Leslie had been wearing a dress this morning, he was equally surprised to see elegant Pamela wearing a plain red T-shirt and white shorts. She had probably dressed down for the volleyball workout to please Russ. Even her straight, chestnut brown hair was tied back in a ponytail instead of hanging loose down to her shoulders.

"Now that's more like it," Pam commented when she noticed Jed's healthy low-calorie dinner. "So, how's it going?"

"What? My diet or my love life?"

"Whatever."

"Well, I think maybe I've lost some weight."

Pamela nodded. "I think you're right. It's really beginning to show in your face. And it looks like your arms are firming up, too."

Jed was so pleased by the compliments that he almost put down his fork then and there. But hunger got the better of him.

"So, how is it going in the love department?" Pamela prodded as Jed went back to his salad.

Jed shrugged. "Maybe we should stick to talking about my diet. I seem to be making more progress there."

"Well, don't get discouraged," Pamela assured him. "You'll see. As soon as you lose the weight, you'll be more confident and your whole life will change drastically."

"Yeah, all my clothes will be too big, and I'll have to spend a fortune to buy new ones." Jed picked up the ketchup bottle, whacked the bottom with his hand, and plopped a blob of ketchup on his burger.

"Now, Jed, don't be so negative. That hamburger looks good. I think I'll make myself one," Pamela said, heading into the kitchen.

Just as Jed was picking up his dirty dishes, Tracy and Fury walked into the house.

"Hey, dude, shaka bra?" Fury asked as he spotted Jed.

"Huh?" Jed replied. Then he noticed that his surfer housemate was wearing kelly green high-tops to match his green-spiked hair.

"Shaka bra. What's up besides the surf?" Fury translated.

"You tell me, Fury," Jed said with a grin. "Where have you been keeping yourself? I haven't seen you for a week."

"That makes two of us," Tracy put in.

"Well, the waves have been really bodacious, I mean, rhino, gnarly, awesome, so I've been dropping in on them all week."

"It's nice of you, Fury, to take time out and drop in on us," Tracy said sarcastically.

"How do you like my stone fox? Isn't she raw? I get stoked when I'm near her," Fury said.

Tracy and Jed exchanged glances.

Jed wondered what had happened to the tender, loving couple Tracy and Fury had been earlier in the summer. If he ever got himself a girl friend, Jed promised himself, he'd break up with her before their relationship went downhill. That was certainly the direction in which Tracy's and Fury's seemed to be heading.

Jed sighed. Who was he to talk in the first place, when he didn't even *have* a girl friend? *Please, let me get one,* he told himself, *and I'll do anything to keep her.*

"Hey, gang, I'm home," Russ sang out as he entered the house.

"Where's Chris?" Jed asked.

"Right here," said Chris, a few steps behind Russ. He headed a volleyball up in the air four times in a row.

"Neat trick," Jed complimented him.

"And when we get done with you, you'll be able to do that and more," Russ said. Then he looked over his team. "Great. Everybody's dressed to play. So, let's get started."

Everyone piled out of the house and onto the court Russ had set up earlier in the sand next to the patio.

"Okay, Chris and I will demonstrate what we want you to work on first. Come here, Chris. Let's show them the setup. Then, we're going to work in pairs: me and Pamela, Fury and Tracy, Chris and Jed," Russ instructed.

Boy-girl, boy-girl, boy-boy. When am I going to get a girl? Jed asked himself. Once again he was the odd man out. Everyone would be so tidily paired off if only Leslie would be his girl friend. Jed wasn't giving up on her yet. He'd noticed today that she was becoming increasingly friendly toward him. Or was that just wishful thinking?

Jed snapped out of his thoughts as Chris tossed his ball in the air. As it came down, Russ punched it easily over the net. They made it look so simple, Jed thought.

"Okay, now it's your turn," Russ said, pairing up with Pamela. Chris passed out balls, one to each pair, then joined Jed at the net. He tossed up the ball, as he had done for Russ, and Jed punched it. But Jed's ball landed in the net. Chris threw the ball several more times until one of Jed's balls finally went over. Jed wiped the perspiration from his brow.

"Okay, let's try another exercise," Russ shouted, sounding like a P.E. teacher. "I want you to practice punching the ball to each other. See if you can make twenty-five volleys back and forth."

"Twenty-five? Hey, we got this down," Fury called.

Chris and Jed got their ball going, but five times back and forth was Jed's personal best so far. He struggled to volley the ball back a sixth time, but his arms felt like lead. He must have overdone his workout with the weights.

"What's the matter?" Chris asked as Jed struggled to lift his arm.

"My arms and shoulders ache," Jed admitted, feeling ashamed.

"It's all part of the toughening-up process," Chris said with a shrug. "Your muscles are tight, that's all. They'll get stronger with each practice."

"But how am I going to be able to practice all week, if I can't move my arm now?" Jed asked.

"Don't worry. All you need is a hot bath and a massage. You'll be over your aches and pains by tomorrow," Chris assured him. "Now, come on, don't give in to the pain. We're running out of time. You'll have to learn how to work through it."

Chris volleyed the ball toward Jed again. He tried to punch it back, but in spite of his positive attitude, a sharp pain shot up his right arm, and he missed the ball.

But the physical pain wasn't nearly as great as the humiliation he felt when Leslie, who had just arrived home, came outside to watch them.

"Way to go, butterfingers," she shouted. Earlier in the day, Jed had hoped she'd come to watch the practice. But when he heard Leslie ridiculing him for fanning the ball, he almost wished she had stayed out late with Jeff.

Jed's aches and pains didn't get any better when Russ suggested that they put the two drills together.

"Remember, the secret of volleyball is teamwork," Russ coached, encouraging his players to pass up the ball.

"Oh, so that's the big secret. Now our lifeguard team will really be worried," Leslie teased her brother.

"Go away. You're spying on us," he shouted back.

Leslie headed back into the house. "Don't get all worked up, big brother," she called snidely over her shoulder.

Jed was actually glad she was gone. Jeff's nasty attitude must have rubbed off on her.

"Don't mind Leslie," Russ apologized for his sister. "Competition brings out the worst in her. You guys are doing great. And we're going to practice every evening until you get this game down."

"Every night? When will I have time to do my nails?" Pamela said teasingly.

"You won't need time to do your nails. By the end of this week you won't have any," Russ told her. "But for now I think you've all had enough. Besides, it's getting too dark to see the ball."

Russ's words were music to Jed's ears. He had had enough, more than enough, all right. He couldn't wait to get upstairs and into a nice, hot bath as Chris had advised.

"Hey, by the way," Russ added as Jed was about to go in, "I saw Jeff today and we've set a date for the game. I hate to tell you guys, but The Great V-Ball Challenge is only five days away. We're playing the lifeguards on Saturday afternoon."

"*This* Saturday? There's no way we'll be ready by then," Tracy protested.

"So what's the rush?" Fury asked.

Russ shrugged. "I don't know. Jeff sure seems in a big hurry to play us all of a sudden. But I'm not worried. What difference does it make if we crush them this Saturday or the one after? When you guys are done with my volleyball crash course this week, trust me. You'll be ready. The lifeguards may talk tough, but we're going to play tough. So, I'll see you all same time, same place, tomorrow."

Although Russ seemed pretty confident that he could whip his sad sack of a team into shape in time to not only play, but beat, the lifeguard squad next Saturday, Jed had a pretty good idea why Jeff was in such a hurry to play so soon. The challenge was no longer a grudge match between Russ and Jeff over Jeff's embarrassing loss a couple of weeks ago. It was between Jeff and him—and Jeff couldn't wait to use his head as the volleyball. *Well, the feeling is mutual,* Jed thought as he headed back into the house.

As he walked through the living room, he spotted Leslie lounging on the peach couch. Was she waiting for him? he wondered. He thought about confronting her about her lousy attitude earlier, but he doubted that that would improve things between them.

"I'm sorry I made fun of you out there," Leslie said quickly. "I don't know what got into me." She sighed. "I guess I'm just feeling pretty confused."

Jed shrugged, trying to stay cool. "Want to talk about it?"

Leslie nodded. "Sure."

So, she *had* been waiting around to talk to him, Jed realized, his heart beating faster. He was also glad to know he wasn't the only one feeling a little mixed up. "Mind if I sit down?" Jed asked.

"Oh, sorry, sure." Leslie moved her legs off the couch to make room for him.

"It's hard having dual allegiances," she began. "I mean, on one hand I owe it to the lifeguards to play for them. I mean, I really do want to. But on the other hand, I'll be playing against my own brother and housemates. And when I saw you practicing with Chris, part of me wanted to be there working out with you tonight. So, I guess I just reacted to being pulled in two directions by being bitchy to all of you," she finished.

"I understand," Jed sympathized, feeling relieved. Things weren't as bad as he had thought between them. But Alex had made more headway with Leslie today than he had.

Alex! That was it! The kid had given Jed another brilliant idea. "Listen, Leslie," he said, "I'm willing to forget all the nasty things you said if you are."

"I'll go for that," Leslie said quickly.

"Well, I promised Alex I'd take him to the Fun Zone sometime soon," Jed began while he still had Leslie's undivided attention. "But he's so hyper that I don't think I could handle him there all by myself. I know he really likes you and would listen to you. Do you think you could come with us?"

Leslie nodded. "Sure. He's a neat kid. I really like him, too."

Jed had never thought of Alex as being neat, but if Leslie felt that way about him, well, maybe he would reconsider. "When can you go?" he asked.

"I'm not off again until Friday," Leslie replied.

"Friday's great. I can hold the outing over Alex's head all week. If he's not good, then I'll tell him he can't go."

Leslie laughed. "Well, I'm counting on going. How can that adorable little redhead not behave?" Leslie asked.

"Believe me, you don't know Alex as well as I do." Why was he contradicting her, and maybe talking her out of going? "I mean, you're right, he's a great kid, especially around you," Jed quickly corrected himself.

"So it's a date. The Fun Zone on Friday," Leslie said.

"A date?" Jed had to make sure he'd heard her correctly.

"Well, what would *you* call it?" Leslie replied, confusing Jed more than ever. The last time he had suggested that they had an actual "date," she had balked at the word.

"I'll call it a date, if you want," he answered hesitantly.

"Well, that's better than calling it an outing. Unless you'd like to consider it a field trip," Leslie added with a smirk.

"Okay, then, we've got a field trip on Friday," Jed said. Suddenly he found himself at a loss for words. "Well, I'd better get upstairs. My muscles are really sore. I need a hot bath."

"You looked like you were struggling a bit out there," Leslie said, sounding concerned.

Jed grinned. "I was. Between working out with my weights and Russ's volleyball workout, I'm a mass of aches and pains," he admitted.

"I've got just the remedy for you," Leslie replied. "A massage. Take off your shirt."

Jed did a double take. "What did you say?" he asked, not sure he had heard Leslie right.

She looked a little annoyed. "You heard me. Now come here so I can rub your shoulders."

She didn't have to repeat herself. Jed whipped off his T-shirt and moved closer to her on the couch. The next thing he knew, Leslie was kneading her strong fingers into his shoulder blades, his neck, up and down his arms. As she massaged his tight muscles, he could feel them relax. Her touch was soothing, and suddenly he wasn't quite so jealous of Alex anymore.

Chapter 13

Fury served a practice ball deep into the back court. Tracy dug hard and got under it.

"Pass it up, pass it up!" Russ coached from the sidelines.

Tracy, heeding Russ's advice, bumped the ball up from the back line. Pamela, who was playing center, punched Tracy's ball up in the air with her fist, setting it up perfectly for Jed in the front line. He sprang into the air and smashed the ball over the net the way he had seen Russ and Chris do it a thousand times.

"Great save, Tracy! That's teamwork, Pamela. Nice jump, Jed, real nice! I'm impressed. You're all looking terrific out there!" Russ praised them from the patio.

The fact that he had really gotten his two

feet off the ground surprised Jed as much as it did Russ. Only four nights ago at their first workout, when Jed was all musclebound, he had wondered how Coach Stevens could be so sure that their team would crush Jeff's next Saturday. And now Jed was willing to place money on who would win. Right now he felt they had a slightly better than fifty-fifty chance of winning the game, about as much of a chance as he thought he had of winning Leslie. Russ, Jed had to admit, had actually shaped them all into a half-decent team.

Jed, of course, had more than his share of reasons to want to whip the lifeguard squad. His strong sense of purpose, as well as Russ's and Chris's enthusiasm and understanding of the game, had quickly rubbed off on everybody else. In four short days of intensive practice, Fury had mastered the serve, Tracy had learned how to receive, Pamela had gotten the hang of the setup, and Jed had gotten down the spike and the block.

Although they all seemed to have their specialities, for the last two practice sessions Russ had rotated them around to ensure that each of them could play any position. Tonight Jed felt they were finally coming together as a well-balanced team. But until the game was played and won, Jed knew they couldn't rest on their laurels—or on their rear ends, for that matter. Russ had reminded them of that fact several times when they had dropped onto the warm sand, complaining that they were all pooped out.

But even after the sun sank into the ocean and Russ called it quits for the day, Jed felt full of energy. All week, as well as knocking himself out at Russ's volleyball practices, he had stayed on his diet and weight-training program.

Leslie, unfortunately, hadn't been around the house to give Jed any more massages after Monday night, but Chris had suggested he rub some Ben-Gay into his sore muscles after each practice session. Now, as Jed bounded upstairs to his room two steps at a time, he knew that, as a result of his daily regimen, he had toughened up. Along with his volleyball skills, his stamina had vastly improved.

Jed had no idea where this week had gone. If it hadn't been for the fact that Alex had been asking Jed every day if the next day was Friday, he wouldn't have believed it was already Thursday. When he woke up tomorrow, he'd be taking the kid and—more important— Leslie to the Fun Zone.

Holding the trip over Alex's head had worked like a charm. He had had no idea that the brat could, if he wanted to, be so good. If Alex's new behavior all week was any indication, Jed figured that he had it made in the shade for tomorrow. When then got to the Fun Zone, he could pay more attention to Leslie and a lot less, hopefully, to Alex. When he had his arm around Leslie and Alex under his thumb, then, for sure, he'd admit that Alex was an okay kid.

Even though Jed wasn't all that tired, he knew that the next day would be a long day. He decided to take it easy the rest of the night and just read for a while. After washing up and getting into his pajamas, he got into bed and turned to the section on volleyball in his sports encyclopedia.

All the while he was reading about the history, the rules, and the fine points of the game, Jed kept listening for Leslie to come in the front door. Soon he grew incredibly sleepy, but he couldn't help wondering why Leslie still wasn't home yet. She'd been coming home late all week, in fact, and when Jed had had nothing better to think about while he was baby-sitting, he had speculated on how and where she was spending her time.

Even though Jed hadn't seen her around the house in the evenings since their little chat in the living room, he didn't think that Leslie was purposely avoiding him. Maybe, Jed mused, just on the verge of dropping his book, after her scene on Monday night, she was working out with Jeff and the other lifeguards at some of their own practice sessions. He nodded off, thinking that he, not Jeff, had a date with Leslie tomorrow. With that pleasant thought, he fell asleep with a smile on his face.

Jed woke up at eight-thirty, still smiling. As soon as he popped up in bed, even before his feet hit the floor, he wanted to shout "Thank God it's Friday," but he had to contain his excitement so as not to wake up Russ. Instead he went over to his dresser and took out a new striped short-sleeve shirt instead of his usual T-shirt.

After slipping into his jeans, he discovered that he had something else to shout about. His middle didn't droop over the top of them at all. The jeans were, in fact, too big on him. On Saturday morning, if he went into town as soon as the stores opened, he'd have time to buy a new pair of jeans before their final practice session before the big game. Now that he had lost some weight, Jed hoped that he could at last get into a trendier pair of tighter fitting, faded black jeans, the kind that all the guys wore.

But for today, he'd have to make do with his old, generic jeans and a belt. He walked back to the dresser and splashed some of Russ's after-shave lotion on his face. Today wasn't just any old day with Alex at the beach.

Jed picked up his wallet and his car keys and grabbed his watch from the night table, strapping it onto his wrist as he raced downstairs. When he hit the hall, it still came as a shock to Jed to find Leslie, up and about and ready to go out with him. If the sundress she was again wearing was any sign, it seemed that she wanted to look especially nice this time for him.

"Have you had breakfast?" Jed asked, hoping she had.

"Yep. What about you?"

"Oh, I'll get something later. We'd better get going," Jed replied, willing to sacrifice breakfast to spend as much of the day with Leslie as possible.

"Maybe we should take my car," he added as they stepped outside. "Alex is used to it."

"Okay. Then I can entertain him on the drive down," Leslie agreed as they got into the van.

Jed wished that the seven-year-old had a driver's license so that he and Leslie could sit in the backseat together. He stole a sideways glance in her direction, and she threw him a smile. Jed looked away quickly, feeling a little embarrassed.

Jed pulled up in front of the Hartman house, picked up Alex and belted the little boy in the front seat. Almost as soon as they were underway, Alex started bouncing up and down in his seat, straining the belt. "We're going to the Fun Zone, we're going to the Fun Zone, we're going to the Fun Zone," he chanted like a broken record, using the front seat as a trampoline.

Jed wondered how and why he had ever gotten the impression that Alex would be calmer today. Besides belting him in, Jed wished he had bound and gagged him.

"Stop jumping around, Alex. I can't drive if you do that," Jed reprimanded him. "Time to entertain him," he said to Leslie, keeping his eyes on the road as he turned onto the Pacific Coast Highway.

"Let's sing some songs, Alex," Leslie suggested like a skilled camp counselor.

"Okay. How about Old MacDonald? Old MacDonald had a farm, e-i-e-i-o . . ." Alex began without any further encouragement.

"I hate that song," Jed cut in. "Can you sing something else?"

"How about 'There Was An Old Lady Who Swallowed a Fly'?" Leslie offered.

Alex didn't object. Jed had no objections, either, but as the song went into its twentieth verse and the cow swallowed the goat, he wondered if he'd ever get a chance to say anything to Leslie before they reached the Fun Zone parking lot.

As it turned out, he didn't. But at least Alex

had been amused the whole trip. They didn't sing the last verse and kill off the old lady until Jed cut the ignition.

Once everyone was out of the car, Jed figured he would take Alex by one hand and Leslie by the other. But he was wrong. All wrong. As soon as they started walking toward the amusement park, Alex grabbed Leslie and pulled her toward the ticket booth. Hand in hand, they ended up running all the way there, with Jed jogging right behind them.

"I want to go on all the rides," Alex shouted as they reached the booth.

Jed was relieved to learn that Alex wasn't afraid of any of them. But, once again, he was wrong. As soon as Jed had bought the kid an unlimited ride wristband and suggested that they all go on the Pirate Ship, he found out what Alex meant by "all the rides."

"I don't want to go on the Pirate Ship. It's scary when it swings back and forth. I only want to go on *my* rides," Alex explained.

"What are your rides?" Leslie asked patiently.

"The kiddie rides. You know, like Bulgy the Whale."

"Bulgy the Whale," Jed repeated, underwhelmed by the prospect of spending his whole day watching Alex circle in slow motion in a miniature whale.

"Come on, Jed, let's take Alex on his rides. Then we'll go on some of ours. Isn't that right, Alex?" Leslie asked, obviously trying some child psychology.

"I like that idea," Alex agreed readily, taking Leslie's hand again.

What had started as a way to talk Leslie into going with him to the Fun Zone was rapidly turning into a very practical idea. Leslie, Jed observed, had Alex wrapped around her finger. If only the kid would allow him some time to wrap his arm around Leslie.

But for now, if Jed had any hopes of taking Leslie on some rides, he had no choice but to go for the compromise. The next thing he knew, he was strapping Alex onto a black and red motorcycle and listening to him beep its horn as the little cars and motorcycles went around and around in a boring circle. When the Jeepers Beepers ride was over, Alex was all revved up and ready for the next ride, the Jet Copters. Alex showed his wristband to an attendant and climbed into a royal blue plane. Jed and Leslie watched Alex from below as he used the controls to make the plane go up and down.

"That was great! I want to go again," Alex said, his eyes beaming as brightly as the flashing lights he had turned on and off in the helicopter.

"No repeats," Jed said sternly, leading Alex over to the Red Baron, another airplane ride. If Alex went on all the kiddie rides more than once, he and Leslie would never get to go on any of their own. But by the time Alex had finished with every kiddie ride in the park, Jed felt dizzy just from watching him.

"Now it's our turn. We're going to go on the Wave Jammer," Jed said firmly, even though his stomach felt a little queasy.

"Okay, Jed," Alex said agreeably. After going on fifteen rides, Jed wasn't at all surprised that he was willing to hold up his end of the bargain. The only question in Jed's mind was whether *he* would hold up on the whirling Wave Jammer.

"Now, listen, Alex, I want you to wait for us right here. Don't go anywhere else or talk to *anyone* else," Leslie lectured as they reached the exit for the ride. "This is where we'll be getting out in just a few minutes. Okay?"

Alex nodded.

"What does that mean?" Leslie asked, obviously trying to stay on the safe side.

"I understand," Alex assured her.

"Come on, Leslie. The line's starting to move," Jed said, pointing toward the entrance to the ride.

A few minutes later, he was buckling them both into a car the shape of a surfboard. The car itself hung from a tilted wheel, and behind them was a brightly colored billboard painted in a surf motif. The Beach Boys started blasting from loudspeakers as the wheel began to spin upward. As the ride picked up speed, the cars started swinging back and forth and the palm trees and surfers on the billboard became a blur. Leslie's screams in Jed's ear drowned out the music, and the next thing he knew she had thrown her arms around him.

They huddled together as their car swung out and back, faster and faster. Leslie's arms were cinching him tighter than the belt around his waist, and Jed wished that the ride would go on forever. But the minute he made the wish, of course, the ride slowed down, and Leslie let go of him. Her screaming subsided and the music slowed down, too. Now Jed could hear the lyrics to "The Girls on the Beach," interpreting the words as a personal message to him. He looked over at Leslie, wanting to kiss her then and there, while he still had his arms around her, but he couldn't work up the courage. Reluctantly, he dropped his arms and helped Leslie out of the car.

As they filed out of the ride, Jed thought he recognized the girl just ahead of him. She was walking arm and arm with a guy, obviously her boyfriend. He'd only gotten a brief glimpse of her when she turned her head, but even still, he thought he'd seen her before somewhere. All of a sudden it occurred to him who she was. Emily, of course. Now Jed understood why she had been so cool to him the day Alex and Mark had fought on the beach. It wasn't that she had found Jed so unappealing. She had had someone else in her life all along! Jed, in a hurry to meet Alex, quickened his pace and caught up to her.

"Hi, Jed," Emily said when she recognized him.

"Oh, Emily," Jed said casually, taking Leslie's hand. He couldn't resist showing Emily that he was with someone, too.

"I thought I saw Alex waiting outside," she said, glancing at Leslie.

"He is. That's why I'm in a hurry. You never know what Alex will do next," Jed said.

"I know what you mean," Emily sympathized. "Mark's been a real handful lately, too. Thank goodness he's at camp for two weeks, but he'll be back tomorrow." She made a face.

Leslie gave Jed a look that clearly indicated she wanted to know what was going on. "Oh, sorry, Leslie," Jed said quickly. "This is Emily."

"And this is Tom," Emily said, introducing her friend, who nodded to them. "Maybe we can try again and get the boys together on the beach again, Jed—say, Tuesday morning?"

"Great. Same place as last time, ten

o'clock," Jed suggested. Now that Emily had made it clear that she was attached, she obviously felt comfortable about bringing the boys together again. *Well, maybe by Tuesday, I'll be attached to someone, too,* Jed thought. It didn't hurt to hope.

"Ten o'clock sounds fine. See you then," Emily agreed, and she and Tom headed down the boardwalk.

"What took you so long? The ride ended ten minutes ago," Alex shouted, running through the crowd toward Jed and Leslie.

"I ran into someone we know. Remember Emily, Mark's baby-sitter? We're going to get together with them again next week."

"See? I knew there'd be a next time, Jed," Alex gloated.

"What'll we do now?" Jed asked, anxious to change the subject.

"Let's go on something a little slower," Leslie suggested.

"That ride looked scary," Alex put in.

"It was," Jed admitted. "But I've got just the ride for us. The Cave Train. It's really slow."

"Sounds good to me," Leslie said.

"You'll like it, too, Alex," Jed added. "It has cavemen, dinosaurs, and all sorts of wild animals inside."

"Dinosaurs? Let's go, Jed." Alex gave a whoop and started jumping up and down.

What Jed didn't tell Leslie or Alex was that the train went through a dark tunnel. By promising he'd buy him a double-scoop ice-cream cone after the ride, Jed persuaded Alex to sit in the car behind him and Leslie. As the car entered the tunnel, Jed put an arm around Leslie's shoulder. She didn't object. In fact, as soon as a caveman popped out of a hole and swung a club at them, her arms were back around Jed. They came around a curve and into a black abyss.

Leslie cuddled in close to Jed. "You smell nice," she whispered in his ear.

"So do you," Jed whispered back.

"It's really dark in here. I'm not scared, though," Alex called out bravely from the car behind them.

Neither Jed nor Leslie answered him. They couldn't because their lips were pressed together. Jed half expected Leslie to push him away, but she seemed quite willing to stay just as they were. Alex, fortunately, got very quiet.

"Wow," Leslie said softly when they finally took a breath.

Jed, feeling encouraged to kiss her again, drew Leslie toward him. This time their lips didn't part until after the ride ended. Their car came out of the tunnel into the daylight.

"What are we doing?" Leslie cried, seemingly jolted back into reality by the glare. She drew away from Jed, rubbed her eyes, and looked up at him as if she had just made a big mistake. Jed could tell by the expression on her face that she was somewhat embarrassed over the fact that she had just made out with him in the tunnel.

"I'm not sure what happened. All I know is that I'd like to do it again. What about you?" Jed asked with a grin.

"I'm not sure what's going on, either. I'm all confused. I'm *supposed* to be going with Jeff," Leslie said miserably.

"I've got an idea," Jed said. "Why don't we let Alex decide? If he's up for another ride, we'll do it again." Jed winked at Leslie, then asked Alex over his shoulder, "Hey, Alex, want to go on the Cave Train again? Or do you want your ice cream now?"

Alex didn't answer.

Jed turned around. "So what's it going to be, kiddo?"

Again, Alex said nothing. He couldn't, because he was no longer there.

Chapter 14

"Alex, don't be cute. We know you're down there on the floor," Leslie said.

Jed frowned and vaulted out of his car to check. No luck. His heart dropped. "We'd better go look for him," Jed said, and he and Leslie raced back to the Cave Train entrance. "Did you see a little kid with red hair come out of here?" Jed asked the mustached ride attendant.

"You mean the cute little guy with freckles? I saw him go in with you, but I haven't seen him since. Why? Is he lost?" The young man looked concerned.

"He wasn't with us when the ride stopped," Leslie told him.

"Wait here. I'll go look in all the cars," the attendant said, taking off.

"I can't believe it. How could Alex just disappear?" Jed threw up his hands in disgust. He was really worried now.

"Maybe you shouldn't have let him sit by himself," Leslie began.

"Oh, so now it's all my fault." Jed glared at her.

"You *are* responsible for him, Jed," Leslie replied evenly.

"It's not like I didn't tell you that he was a handful," Jed said, exasperated. "Now you can see why I asked you to come along to help me with him in the first place."

"No way, Jed. I'm not going to let you put the blame on *me*," Leslie answered. "You were the one who made him sit back there. Besides, you know as well as I do that my helping you out with Alex wasn't the only reason you wanted me to come here. So let's not get into a big fight about it, okay?"

"You knew that all along?" Jed asked, more puzzled now than angry.

"Of course," Leslie replied. "Sure, I like Alex, but did you really think I'd go to the Fun Zone with you just for his sake?"

"Yeah, I guess I did," Jed mumbled. "Or at least until we went into the Cave Train." He looked around impatiently. "What's taking that guy with the bushy mustache so long, anyway?"

Almost immediately, the attendant reappeared. "He's not in there," he reported. "You'd better go tell Lost and Found that he's missing right away. It's next to the ticket booth where you came in."

"Thanks for looking," Jed said, turning to Leslie. "Let's go." He grasped her by the hand and the two of them raced down the boardwalk toward Lost and Found.

"Hey, Leslie!" someone shouted as they fled past the entrance of the Penny Arcade.

Leslie slowed her pace a bit to see who had called her. Jed was forced to come to a stop as the girl called again, "In here, Leslie."

The girl had short, wild red hair, just a shade lighter than Alex's, and she was trying to roll her last black ball into a hole for three-of-a-kind at a Pokereno game.

"Hi, Rain," Leslie replied. "Listen, I can't talk now. Alex, the little kid Jed baby-sits, just got lost. Oh, sorry, this is Jed."

"Come on, Leslie, we're losing time," Jed reminded her.

"See you at the game tomorrow," Leslie called over her shoulder as Jed pulled her by the arm again. A few minutes later, they were inside the Lost and Found shack, and Jed was trying to catch his breath as he gave a security guard Alex's description.

"If he shows up here, we'll page you over the loudspeaker system," the uniformed guard told Jed after he had finished writing all of the information down.

"Okay. Thanks," Jed replied. Then he turned to Leslie. "Where do you think we should look next?"

Leslie shrugged. "Back at the van?"

Jed nodded. "What do we have to lose?" They dashed out of the shack, down the boardwalk, and across the parking lot to the van, but there was no sign of Alex.

"If we don't find him soon, I think we should file a missing-child report with the police," Jed said, really panicked now. He tried not to think of the consequences.

"Wait a second, I've got an idea," Leslie said.

Jed barely heard her. The first thing the police would do, he knew, would be to contact Alex's parents. And as soon as Mr. Hartman learned of the situation, he would be absolutely furious. He remembered now that Mrs. Hartman had been really understanding and hadn't blamed Jed when Alex had fallen off the pier one day, but her husband hadn't been nearly as tolerant.

"Maybe he went back on one of the kiddie rides," Leslie was saying. "All he has to do to get back on a ride is show his wristband to an attendant."

"That's it!" Jed snapped his fingers. "Why didn't I think of that? Alex wanted to go on the Jet Copter again. What are we waiting for?" He broke into a run one more time across the asphalt parking lot, with Leslie at his heels. They headed back down the boardwalk to the Jet Copter ride at the far end of the park. Jed scanned the ride above as he tried to catch his breath, but even wearing sunglasses, the glare of the midday sun bouncing off the metal bodies of the planes prevented him from seeing much. He and Leslie had to wait until the ride stopped and the kids disembarked from their helicopters.

"There he is!" Jed shouted. He jumped the gate that separated the ride from the boardwalk, weaved past several surprised kids and their parents, and hurried up to Alex. Leslie was right behind him.

"Why did you go off without us?" Jed practically screamed. "Why didn't you tell us where you were going?" Alex looked startled by his sudden appearance and his loud voice.

"I didn't want to interrupt anything," Alex explained. "You and Leslie were busy doing what my mom and dad do sometimes, and they don't like it if I interrupt them."

Jed shook his head in disbelief at what Alex had just told him, then grabbed hold of his small hand.

"You're hurting my hand," Alex protested.

"I don't care," Jed answered. "I'm going to make sure you don't disappear on me again. You're going to hold my hand the rest of the day or we're going home." He wished he could put a handcuff instead of an unlimited-ride band on one of Alex's wrists.

But as he scolded Alex, he was also silently admonishing himself. He knew full well that if he had paid more attention to Alex and less to Leslie, the kid wouldn't have gotten lost. His tone softened. "What do you want for lunch?"

Alex brightened. "A corn dog, a soda, and an ice-cream cone to start," Alex responded immediately.

Jed sighed as he and Leslie headed down the boardwalk toward the food stands with Alex in tow. Was there any way this day could become any crazier?

Chapter 15

After Alex wolfed down his food, finishing the meal with saltwater taffy and a messy candied apple, it seemed to Jed that he spent the rest of the afternoon taking Alex to the bathroom to wash his hands and face. In between trips, he and Leslie took turns holding on to Alex and going on some of the tamer rides.

It was close to six o'clock when the three of them staggered, dizzy and exhausted, back to the van. They all piled in and headed the thirty miles up the coast to Marina Bay. When Jed was two blocks away from the center of town and the volleyball courts, Leslie said, "You can drop me off here, if you don't mind."

"Aren't you going home?" Jed blurted out in disbelief.

Leslie shrugged. "We've got a volleyball workout tonight, so I'll see you later. But, thanks, Jed, for a wonderful day." Then she hopped out of the van, waved good-bye to Alex, and ran down the beach to the volleyball court. Driving past the area a few minutes later, Jed spotted the lifeguard team. Jeff, Rain, and three beefy lifeguard Jeff-clones whom Jed didn't know by name were already gathered. As the van crawled by the court, he saw Leslie join the group and give Jeff a big smile. Then the six of them split into teams and got serious. From the few hits he saw, Jed thought the team looked pretty strong. He was tempted to park the van and watch them practice for a while longer, but Alex, fidgeting in the seat beside him, reminded him that he'd better take the kid straight home.

Driving back to Alex's house, Jed was really mad at himself. One thing he didn't need to be a genius to figure out was why Leslie had wanted to be dropped off there. It was ridiculously obvious that she still cared for Jeff and didn't want him to know how she had spent her day off.

But how could Leslie skip off to her volleyball practice as if she had no feelings for him at all, as if nothing out of the ordinary had happened in the Cave Train? Jed wondered as he turned onto Alex's street. Because nothing had. It had been a simple case of mistaken identity!

He pulled up in front of the Stevens's house, unbuckled Alex, and walked him to the door.

"Thanks, Jed, for taking me to the Fun Zone!" Alex said. "And good luck with Leslie. I think she likes you."

Jed smiled. "Yeah, sure. I'll see you on Monday."

"Maybe Leslie will be your girl friend by then," Alex said cheerily. Then he walked through the front door.

Jed trudged back to the van, tired and downhearted, wishing he could believe what Alex had just said. But Jed knew better than to put much faith in the words of a pint-sized little brat.

After a full day of adventures at the Fun Zone with Alex and Leslie, Jed needed some sleep. He went upstairs, threw off his sneakers and jeans, and sacked out for the night as soon as he arrived home.

He awoke the next morning in a much better mood. It looked as if he probably would never manage to persuade Leslie to be his girl friend, and certainly not by Monday, as Alex had predicted. But one thing Jed knew for sure: Even if Russ's team didn't stand a chance against the brawny lifeguards, he, for one, was going to go all out to beat them.

Then Jed remembered that he wanted to go into town to buy himself a better fitting pair of jeans. He got ready to go hurriedly and decided he'd grab something to eat at the Surf-rider Cafe before the stores opened.

Even though it was after nine when Jed came downstairs, not one of his housemates was stirring. They're conserving their energy for the big game, Jed thought as he tiptoed out of the house.

By the time he got into town, he realized he was pretty hungry. Now that he thought about it, he had good reason to be. He had hardly eaten at all yesterday.

Entering the cafe, it amazed him what little importance food had had in his life lately. Since going on his diet, he no longer lived to eat.

He ordered his breakfast, then carried his tray over to an empty table by the window. From there he was able to see Jeff heading toward the cafe. As soon as he came through the door, Jeff spotted Jed, too. He approached Jed's table.

"You always show up, don't you, Mason?" Jeff said. "Once again, you're just the person I was hoping to run into today."

"Have a seat," Jed replied with a shrug. He could be civil, even if Jeff wasn't.

"Why don't *you* stand up?" Jeff growled. "Or

better yet, let me help you." He tried to pull Jed by his arm, but got a handful of his white T-shirt instead. The sleeve ripped, but Jed remained in his chair until he got to his feet on his own. "Take your hands off me," he said evenly.

"Not until you take your hands off my girl. I know you two spent the day together at the Fun Zone." Jeff looked as if he might punch him.

"What makes you so sure she's your girl?" Jed wasn't at all sure Leslie was his, either, but he was certain that Rain must have told Jeff that she had seen them together at the amusement park.

"Don't be such a wise guy," Jeff said, giving Jed a shove.

This time Jed wasn't going to let Jeff get rough with him. "Watch who you're pushing," he said, retaliating with a shove back. Jed was surprised at his own strength. From the look on his face as he tumbled backward slightly from the force of the push, so was Jeff.

"Hey, break it up! No fighting in here," the man called from behind the counter.

Jed sat down again to eat his breakfast, but he was too angry now to eat. Jeff walked over to the counter to order himself a cup of coffee to go. As he left, he called over to Jed, "Don't worry, dude. I'll get you later when we whip your butt on the volleyball court."

"I'm really worried," Jed called back. He timed it, however, so that he said it just after Jeff had left the cafe. Then he went back to eating his breakfast. Now he had a nervous stomach. He kept picturing Jeff smashing the ball at his head. Finally, Jed picked up the glass of juice, downed it, and took a piece of toast with him on his way out of the cafe. He walked to the corner and crossed Windward Way, anxious to try on a pair of sharp-looking, stonewashed black jeans. Things were going to have to start improving—and soon.

Chapter 16

"Jed, I can't believe that's you," Leslie squealed as he stepped out onto the sun-filled deck wearing his new clothes. The whole team minus Chris was outside and ready to play volleyball. In fact, Jed realized, they had probably all been waiting for him to come home to begin their final practice before the big game.

"You look fantastic," Pamela said. "You must have dropped at least ten pounds to get into those jeans."

"Fifteen as of this morning." Jed shrugged as if it were no big deal. "I weighed myself on the drugstore scale in town."

"Way to go, Jed," Russ said approvingly, giving him five. Jed slapped his open hand.

"That denim jacket looks great on you," Leslie said.

Jed was surprised that Leslie was taking such an interest in how he looked. Why was she still hanging around the house? It was almost one o'clock. He would have thought that she'd be working out at the courts in town with the guards by now.

"It really does. I still can't get over how different you look," Pamela went on.

"Thanks, guys," Jed said. "But I couldn't have done it without everyone's support and encouragement. Pamela got me on the diet, Russ developed the weight-training program, Leslie . . ."

"Okay, Jed. Cut the speech and the fashion show," Russ broke in. "You can't practice in tight jeans, so hurry up and change. We've got a game to get ready for."

Leslie, apparently taking Russ's remark as her cue to leave, followed Jed inside.

"Well, good luck," she said with a smile. "I'll see you later. May the best team win."

When Jed emerged again a few minutes later in his loose-fitting gym shorts, Tracy was brandishing a large plastic sack.

"What's in the bag? A present for me?" Jed joked.

"No, a present for all of us. I made these up at the store," Tracy replied. Then she took out a half dozen one-size-fits-all T-shirts with "We're a Team" printed on the front and "Pass It Up" on the back.

"Wow, these are terrific," Pamela exclaimed, taking one of the shirts and slipping it over her tank top. Everyone followed her example.

"I was going to give you guys a little pep talk, but I guess you've already gotten the message," Russ said. "Thanks, Tracy, your shirts are great."

She grinned. "I've got something else for everyone."

"More presents? I like presents," Fury said as Tracy passed out red volleyball visors that matched the lettering on their shirts.

"Okay," Russ said. "If we play as good as we look, we'll have a good chance of bageling the lifeguards. Now let's get out on the court!"

After an hour's practice session in the hot afternoon sun, Russ finally decided that his team had had enough. He didn't want to wear them out before the game.

Russ beat Jed to the upstairs shower, so Jed sprawled out on his bed to rest. While he waited, he thought about how lucky he was to have such great housemates. Sure, things would be even nicer if Leslie were his girl friend. But, in any case, he considered himself pretty lucky to have four—well, maybe five— housemates who were such good friends.

Chapter 17

"Why don't we take my van?" Jed suggested at four-thirty that afternoon. "Then we'll only have to take one car."

"We should have painted your van red and white," Tracy joked as they all piled in.

"How did red and white come to be our colors?" Pamela asked. Jed started the engine and pulled away from the curb.

"I can answer that," Russ chimed in. "Red is for the blood bath we're going to be giving the lifeguards. And white is for our motto, 'Don't spike until you see the whites of their eyes.'"

"Cute, Russ. Very cute," Jed said over his shoulder, turning onto the highway.

Ten minutes later, he pulled into a parking space right in front of volleyball court number two. The lifeguards weren't around yet since most of them were on duty until five o'clock. Chris, however, was there, waiting for the rest of his team to arrive.

"Hey, where did you guys get those cool shirts and visors?" he asked as soon as everyone came onto the court.

"Tracy got them for us," Russ said, pointing to the lettering on the front and sticking out his chest proudly.

"And I've got a set for you," she told Chris, handing him a shirt and visor. Almost immediately he looked like everyone else.

"Great idea, Tracy! Thanks. Okay, why don't we warm up until the guards arrive? Fury, you serve first," their co-captain called, clapping his hands.

Everyone took their places, Russ and Jed on the front line, Pamela in center, Tracy on the back line, and Fury serving.

"Okay, you know our strategy," Chris said from the other side of the net, where he had positioned himself all week so he could receive and return the ball.

Fury served a dozen or so balls before Chris yelled, "They're coming! But keep practicing until they're on top of us."

Jed knew what Chris was thinking. He wanted the guards to see that their team was not only tough, but together. Jed blocked a ball just as Jeff approached the court.

"Okay, that's it," Russ yelled as the guards gathered on the sidelines.

"Not bad for a wimp," Jeff said loudly to Jed as he stepped out of bounds. "Real cute outfits, too."

"Aren't they?" Jed said, standing right up to him, then turning around so that Jeff could read the back. The guards were all wearing their standard red shorts and yellow guard tank tops.

Jeff snorted and said to Russ, "Let's get started."

"Are you sure you don't need to warm up?" Jed suggested snidely.

"I said, let's get started," Jeff barked back.

"Okay, okay if that's the way you want it," Russ interceded quickly. "Good game." He extended his hand to Jeff.

Jeff let Russ's hand hang there in midair. "Let's go!" he called to his team instead.

All the guards except Leslie formed a huddle on the sidelines.

"Good game, Russ," she said, walking over to shake her brother's hand. "I'm sorry Jeff has turned this into a grudge game. But I don't think the grudge is against you anymore. Since Jed has been spending some time with me, Jeff seems to really have it in for him."

Russ raised his eyebrows. "With good reason?"

Leslie shrugged. "I don't know. Maybe. Let's forget about it right now, okay? Play your best."

"Thanks, Les. You, too."

Leslie nodded to Jed and walked over to her team.

"Heads or tails," Jeff said, rejoining them.

"Heads," Russ said.

Jeff took a quarter out of his pocket, flipped the coin, and let it drop into the sand. Then he bent to see how the coin had landed. "Heads it is. Your serve," he called out gruffly.

Jed had to restrain himself from whooping out loud. They had hoped to win the toss so they could serve first.

"Okay, on the court," Russ directed his team.

They took their places opposite four hulks, one in each corner of their court, and the two girls positioned in the middle.

"Serve 'em up," Jeff called to Russ.

Russ rolled the ball to Fury and gave him a thumbs-up sign.

Fury clenched his fist and punched the ball over the net low and hard. One of the guys in the front line tried to block it back, but netted it instead. He rolled the ball back under the net to Fury.

"One-nothing," Fury called out, serving the ball again. It was 6–0, in favor of Russ's team, before Fury's hand got tired and he slapped a ball into the net.

Jed knew that their strategy, to jump ahead by having Fury serve first, had worked well. Now it was the blond-haired guard in the right-hand corner serving. He racked up three points for the guards before the ball changed servers. Russ's team rotated and it was Russ's turn to serve.

"Six–three," Russ shouted before sending two unreturnable serves deep to the guards' back line. Jeff let the ball drop and dived too late for the first serve. Leslie, standing in the middle, missed the second and even more difficult spin serve.

"Come on, let's get with it," Jeff yelled at her.

Leslie cringed. Jed could tell that she didn't like Jeff's tone of voice. Good, he thought. Russ served another ball deep in the court. This time Jeff didn't give Leslie a chance. He jumped in front of her and tried to bump the ball across the net without passing it up. It bounced out of bounds.

"Eight–three. Change sides," Russ said at the midpoint of the game.

"Now you'll have the sun in your eyes," Jeff sneered at Jed as they passed each other. Jed tipped his visor, then took his place on the front line. Russ served another ball, this time to Rain in midcourt. Jeff cut in front of her, stole the ball, and bumped it back over the net to Tracy.

"Pass it up! Pass it up!" everyone chanted in unison.

Heeding her teammates' advice, Tracy passed the ball to Chris, who smashed it sharply over the net.

"We're a team!" Tracy whooped after the ball thunked to the sand for another point.

Once again, Russ served the ball and once again, Jeff was playing everybody's position but his own. He raced up to the front line and blocked Russ's serve to win back the ball.

"Okay, we've got possession," he shouted, trying to rally his team. But by then, he was being such a ball hog that they didn't seem to care. Leslie, Jed noticed, seemed more than turned off at this point.

"You've played every other position, Jeff. Why don't you serve now, too?" she asked sarcastically.

Jeff ignored her and passed the ball to one of his brawny guards, who powered the ball deep for a point. He overshot the court serving his next ball, however, and it was Jed's turn to serve.

When he saw the guards playing him deep, Jed used his brains and marshmallowed the serve. Everyone on Jeff's team stepped aside, expecting Jeff to dig for the ball. Plunk! It landed on the sand just over the net, making the game 9–4. Jed served well twice more, until the score was 11–4.

But by the time it was the lifeguards' turn to serve again, they seemed pretty demoralized. They gave up the ball almost immediately. Chris served out the game for his team, making the win a 15–4 rout.

As Jeff's team headed off the court, Russ gathered his team in a huddle.

"We're a team," they chanted in a whisper, their arms around each other. Their voices became louder with each repetition of the phrase until they were screaming it at the top of their lungs.

To Jed's surprise, Leslie came over to the group at the peak of their shrieking.

"Great playing, you guys," she congratulated them. They quieted immediately.

Russ put his arms around his sister and brought her into the huddle.

"Next time you'll be on *our* team," he told her.

"So how about we all get some pizza and celebrate? My treat," Jed said.

Leslie started to back out of the huddle.

"Hey, where are you going?" Jed said. "We're a team, aren't we?"

Leslie hesitated. "I was kind of hoping you'd say that," she answered, encircling Jed's waist with her arm.

Suddenly, Jeff walked over to Leslie and tapped her on the shoulder. "Come on, Leslie, let's go get something to eat."

"I don't think so, Jeff. I'm sorry, but I'm busy tonight."

"What's that supposed to mean?" Jeff said in surprise. "And since when are we hanging out with other people? I thought we were going together," he added, almost yanking Leslie away from Jed.

Now it was Jed's turn to say, "Hey, take your hands off my girl."

"Since when are you his girl?" Jeff asked Leslie, still holding on to her arm.

"You're hurting me," she protested. Jeff relaxed his grip, and Leslie wrenched herself loose.

"Just answer the question," Jeff boomed.

Jed stepped in front of Leslie. "Bug off, Jeff. Come on, Leslie, let's take a walk. And I advise you, Jeff, to do the same. No hard feelings." Jed turned toward his teammates. "We'll meet you guys over at Fat Slice in a few minutes, okay?"

Jed took Leslie's hand and started walking with her down the beach. Jeff was about to follow when Russ, Chris, and Fury formed a group around him. Jeff scanned the volleyball area to see if any of his lifeguard buddies were still around, but they were long gone. And by the time the threesome escorted Jeff to his car, Jed and Leslie were out of sight, too.

Leslie looked up at Jed. "When Jeff started

yelling at me and hogging everyone's ball, that was the end," she said as some little waves by the water's edge hit their feet. "But I'm glad he did."

"Come on, Leslie, don't tell me you wanted to tank the game," Jed said.

"No, I'd never do that. It was my choice to play for the guards, and I stuck with it. But I guess I was looking for a good excuse to break up with Jeff. And he gave me one."

Jed took her into his arms. "I hope I'm not getting you on the rebound," he said, frowning. "They say rebound romances don't work out, you know."

"Oh, come on, Jed. Couldn't you tell I was falling for you all along?"

Jed shook his head. "I guess not. I was too busy worrying about myself to notice."

"Worrying about what?"

"Well, you know, shaping up, that kind of stuff."

Leslie looked at Jed. "Do you really think that makes any difference to me? I liked you chunky, and I, well, more than like you now, not so chunky." She hesitated. "Just out of curiosity, Jed, when did you first fall for me?"

Jed grinned. "Probably that day after I moved into the beach house, when everyone had that picnic on the beach to get to know one another. It was love at first sight," he answered. "What about you, Leslie?"

"It was the night you taught me how to fix my flat tire," she replied tenderly.

Jed put his arm around Leslie's waist and walked with her into the water until it was up to their thighs. He wanted their first kiss as a couple to be one they'd both remember for a long time, like something out of an old movie. The cool waves lapping at his legs sent a chill over him, but he still felt warm inside. He pulled Leslie toward him, and an instant later their lips were gently touching. It was still too light out for the sun to be setting in the background, but Jed felt the kiss was perfect—even better than in the movies.

"Shaka bra, Tracy?" Fury shouted as he entered the beach house.

Don't you shaka-bra me. I'm not one of your surfing pals, Tracy thought. She was too furious for words. Where did he get his nerve? How could he just stroll in looking like a drowned rat and rattle off that unintelligible surfer slang to her as if nothing were wrong?

It infuriated her even more that he could casually ask her what was happening" when he obviously didn't give a damn.

If Fury didn't get out of his water-logged high-tops and his soaked cut-offs and T-shirt and into his western getup fast, there was no way they would be on time for their next show. Why should she be the one to care so much? Tracy asked herself as she watched some drops of water trickle off the ends of Fury's straggly platinum blond hair and onto the polished, hardwood floor.

Feeling too enraged to speak without screaming at him, she counted to ten, and answered, "You tell me."

Fury shook his head, shaking water onto Tracy and the peach walls in the hall, then slapped the side of his head with his palm. "Oh, yeah. I'm a little late. Me and the guys had a couple of cool Coronas before breaking up." He hit his head again. "I can't get this water out of my ears."

"It must have traveled up to your brain and affected your memory," Tracy said snidely. "Haven't you forgotten something? Like what day it is? What time it is? What happens on Saturday night? Do you even know who I am?"

Jed's and Leslie's timely appearance at the top of the stairs temporarily got Fury off the hook. Tracy turned as they started downstairs. Jed was wearing a brown tweed sports coat, white shirt, tan slacks, and a dark brown knit tie, another new outfit, Tracy supposed. Ever since he'd gone on a diet and workout program and dropped almost twenty pounds, Jed had become an impeccable dresser, purchasing jackets with two pairs of matching slacks. With Leslie on Jed's arm, in a white dress, the handsome couple looked to Tracy like they were in a wedding party. She had to laugh at how Jed's sharp appearance contrasted with that of her own boyfriend's.

"Hey, looking good." Fury flashed Jed and Leslie a big smile as they reached the bottom of the stairs.

"Wish I could say the same for you, Jed returned cheerfully.

Tracy's mouth dropped open. Jed was the only person who could get away with saying anything like that to Fury. If anyone else teased him about how he looked, he hit the ceiling. He was particularly sensitive about his punk-style hair.

Earlier in the summer, however, Jed had won Fury's trust by offering to float him a loan when Russ was pressuring Fury to come up with his share of the rent money. Russ needed fast cash to pay for the repairs to his Suzuki, which he had wrecked the day his parents had gone on vacation to Europe. To pay for the repairs, he had came up with the bright idea of renting out all the rooms in his parents' beach house. That was how they had all come to be living under one roof for the summer in the first place.

So far, Jed had continued to stand by Fury whenever he got into trouble—and that was pretty often. Tracy surmised that after what she was planning on telling him tonight, Fury would soon be turning to him again. Jed would be there for him. That was the kind of guy Jed was. He always gave everybody the benefit of the doubt, which, in Fury's case, Tracy knew from experience, was sometimes hard to do.

"Where are you two heading in those fancy duds?" Fury asked.

"Out to a midnight dinner show in Los Angeles," Jed answered.

"What's the matter with our show at Ports of Call? Too down-home for you?" Fury grinned again.

"I'd love to see you and Tracy perform, Fury, but, obviously, there's no show to go to tonight," Leslie said, eying Fury's disheveled hair and clothes. She turned to Tracy and bit her lip. "Woops. Stuck my foot in my mouth that time."

"And we're not sticking around to help you get it out. We're late already. See you around, Fury. Bye, Tracy," Jed said, pulling Leslie toward the door.

"Be strong," Leslie hissed to Tracy as Jed tugged on her arm.

Tracy gave Leslie a thumbs-up sign. Then she waited until she heard the door slam shut before she started in on Fury again.

"You're late, alright. That's okay if you're the rabbit in *Alice in Wonderland*, but not so good if you have a nine-o'clock show to do. You know, for some reason I'm not even that angry at you for standing me up. But how irresponsible can you get? Lenny must be pulling his hair out by now. And I don't care what dumb excuse you come up with this time." There. She had said it and she meant it.

"I'm sorry, Tracy. I really didn't mean to be late, Fury said. I just didn't realize what time it was. That's the God's honest truth."

It was exactly like Fury, Tracy thought, to worm his way out of this one. By not trying to excuse his behavior. No, she now told herself. Well, she wasn't going to fall for it. She had promised Leslie that she'd be strong. The best thing for her to do now was to end this whole thing clean and simple.

"Look, Fury, I'm tired of yelling at you every time you act like a bad little boy," Tracy began. As much as Leslie had boosted her courage with her little pep talk, breaking up with Fury, Tracy realized, was easier said than done.

"So don't." Fury shrugged.

"Well, you won't have to worry about me ragging you anymore."

"What's that supposed to mean?"

"What do you think?"

"You can't mean what I think you mean."

"Yes, I can," Tracy said firmly.

"Come on, Tracy. I said I was sorry. I know I was late, but you don't have to have a fit over it. I wasn't late on purpose. Look I'll explain to Lenny what happened."

"Even a little kid knows to come home when it gets dark," Tracy argued, ignoring Fury's apology. Then she caught herself. She wasn't going to get into round after futile round of arguments with him, then end up taking him back. If she wasn't careful, he'd be kissing and making up with her before she had a chance to tell him that as a couple they were history. She took a deep breath and remembered what she and Leslie had talked about earlier. She couldn't be a wimp.

"Listen," she told Fury straight out, "if you didn't care enough about me to be on time, at least you could have shown some concern for Lenny. You know as well as I do how dependent he is on our act. Without us, his restaurant will go under. So, to make a long story short, I'm sick and tired of your irresponsible, unreliable, childish behavior. And that's that."

"Are you telling me we're through?"

"You've got it." Tracy was glad that Fury had been the one to say it and not her. She wondered if she actually would have gotten the words out of her mouth.

"Radical. That'll leave me more time to surf," Fury countered. He spun around, spraying Tracy with his wet hair again, and sauntered down the hall. Then he hoisted his surfboard onto his shoulder and headed out the door.

It was obvious to Tracy that Fury was trying to make her believe that he was glad that she had ended their relationship. But she saw through the cover-up. She suspected that underneath his laid-back facade, Fury was hurting as much as she was. She wanted to shout after him that it was dangerous to surf after dark, but then thought better of it. Now that he was out of the house, and, most likely, out of her life, why should she worry about him anymore? She made an effort to push her concern for where Fury was heading now out of her mind. Right now she had more important things to do, like trying to explain to Lenny why they weren't at the restaurant.

As she skulked down the hall toward the portable phone in the kitchen, she knew in her heart that she would rather have called after Fury and begged him to come back than to call Lenny and tell him that they were splitting up their act. Lenny, she knew, would ask what had happened between her and Fury and it would hurt her to explain.

Tracy reluctantly picked up the receiver, dialed the nuber of the restaurant, and got the cashier. As she waited for Lenny to come to the phone, it occurred to Tracy that without Fury to back her up on the bass, she had no act. In the last month, Fury's solo numbers and riffs on bass had become as much of a draw as her country-and-western ballads. For the last few weekends, in fact, they had shared equal billing. Without Fury, Lenny would problably want to drop her act altogether. Part of her almost hoped he would. It wouldn't be the same without Fury, anyway, she thought as Lenny answered the phone.

"Hello, Lenny here."

"Hi, Lenny. This is Tracy."

"Not the Tracy who's supposed to be performing tonight at Ports of Call? You're not canceling on me for the second show are you? I've got it wrong. Please, Tracy, tell me I'm wrong. Tell me you're a different Tracy."

"I'm sorry, Lenny. I wish I could. But Fury never showed up in time to make the first show. Then, when he did come home, we had a fight."

"Spare me the details of your love life and get to the point," Lenny said, much to Tracy's relief.

She was more than glad not to have to tell him about the break up. She took a deep breath. "Okay. We won't be doing our show tonight. Or any other night. We've broken up the act."

Lenny groaned "Oh thanks. I've got a room full of people waiting to be entertained. What about you? Can't you at least be responsible enough to get down here for the next show? I can fire you afterward."

Tracy wondered if Lenny was just kidding around. From the angry tone in his voice, she doubted it. His irritation with her now only pointed out to Tracy how bent out of shape he must have gotten when they hadn't shown up earlier. Still, it wasn't as if she'd deliberately fouled things up for him. He wasn't really being fair. Why should he blame her instead of Fury just because she'd had the decency to phone him?

"Look, Lenny, for the record, Fury was—" she started to say, but cut herself short. What did she have to gain by explaining things to Lenny? It wouldn't change the situation between her and Fury. Besides, with his attitude, Lenny didn't even deserve an explanation.

"I don't think so. Lenny. I don't think I could pull a show off by myself tonight. My heart's not in it." That part was true, all right, Tracy thought as she waited for Lenny's response.

"In that case, Tracy, it's been nice knowing you," he said flatly.

Tracy had to stop herself from slamming the phone down. Wow, next to Fury, Lenny had the shortest memory on record. If it hadn't been for the two of them, his restaurant would have gone under a month after it opened.

"Well, if thats the way you want it," Tracy said aloud.

"Look, Tracy, I'm sorry things had to end this way," Lenny said, obviously hearing the dejection in Tracy's voice. "But you have to admit, it was good while it lasted. Now I've really got to go okay? I've got a restaurant to run. Bye, Tracy."

"Bye Lenny," Tracy said, and hung up the phone.

Between breaking up with Fury and losing the gig, both in the space of an hour, there was only one thing Tracy wanted to do now—head straight up stairs to the sanctuary of her room. As she started toward the comfort of her bed, she couldn't help thinking that what Lenny had just said applied to her and Fury's relationship, too. She was sorry that things had ended the way they had, but she had to admit one thing. It was great while it had lasted.